STAGE SCHOOL

★ Abbi ★
Make or Break

by Geena Dare

 ORCHARD BOOKS

To Amy

ORCHARD BOOKS
96 Leonard Street, London EC2A 4RH
Orchard Books Australia
14 Mars Road, Lane Cove, NSW 2066
ISBN 1 86039 642 9
First published in Great Britain 1998
Paperback original
© Sharon Siamon 1998
The right of Sharon Siamon to be identified as the author
of this work has been asserted by her in accordance with
the Copyright, Designs and Patents Act, 1988. A CIP
catalogue record for this book is available from the
British Library.
Printed in Great Britain

☆CHAPTER ONE☆

I Can't Be Late!

"I'm here. I'm really here. I can't believe it." Abbi Reilly stared at the old brick building through the car window and sighed happily. "The William S. Holly Stage School. Doesn't it look wonderful?"

"Wonderful!" Abbi's mother laughed. Abbi would describe a barn as wonderful when she was excited. "Now you'd better hop out of this car or you'll be late for your audition."

"This is one time I won't be late," Abbi grinned. She had a wide grin that made her cheeks dimple. She whipped the clip off her gold blonde curls, letting them loose around her shoulders. Then she leaned over to peck her mother on the cheek. "Thanks, Mum. You'd better go, too, or you'll miss your appointment." Her mother was an estate agent.

"Have you got everything?" her mum asked, as Abbi struggled to gather up her bag, lunch, umbrella and envelope of school documents.

"Of course, Mum. As if I'd forget anything today!" Abbi said breathlessly. She wormed her way, with all her stuff, out of the front seat of their small red car. "I'll see you at four o'clock," she called over her shoulder. She raced away, clutching her armload of stuff, her gold hair bouncing in the sun.

Abbi's mum looked fondly after her daughter and shook her head. Abbi never walked when she could run. She never spoke quietly when she could shout. At six years old, Abbi had announced that she hated school because they made you sit down and be quiet! Now she was thirteen that opinion hadn't changed. No wonder Abbi was always in trouble at school. Well, maybe a stage school could harness some of Abbi's wild energy, thought her mother, and she crossed her fingers on the steering wheel.

Running up the front steps towards the school doors, Abbi could feel bubbles of excitement welling up inside her. She could hardly wait to walk through those doors. Blair Michaels went to school here; Blair was the star of a weekly television show, and Abbi's idol. Blair Michaels came up these stairs every day – when she wasn't shooting episodes of *My Life*. She wouldn't be here today, of course, because it was summer and the school was just open for auditions, but next term, she might see Blair every day!

Inside the school, Abbi plunged towards the office. Where is everybody? she wondered. The halls seemed awfully quiet. "I'm probably just early." Abbi skidded to a stop, breathless, in front of the main desk.

"Excuse me," she called to a woman working at

a computer. "Where do I go to audition?"

"Audition?" The woman looked up with a puzzled frown. She stared at Abbi's eager face and riveting blue eyes.

"You know, try-outs – auditions. For acting, singing, dancing…" Abbi did a spin in front of the desk, her hair and bag whirling.

"There are no auditions here…" the woman started to explain. "This school is closed for the summer–"

"But they're having auditions *today*. For next year!" Abbi's voice rose. She shoved her William Holly School envelope across the desk.

The woman lowered her glasses and glanced at it. This time her voice was cold. "You're in the wrong place," she said, glaring at the name on the envelope. "The Stage School is at the end of the next block." She stood up and pointed towards the doors. "That way."

"NO!" Abbi wailed, feeling the blood rush from her head. She swayed slightly and clutched the desk for support.

The woman glanced at her white face. "It's only two blocks," she said more kindly. "It's not the end of the world."

"You don't understand." Abbi pointed to the clock above the desk. "It's three minutes to nine. I'll never make it in time."

"Certainly not, if you stand here chattering." The woman returned to her computer screen. "Honestly, you arts students are all alike – so dramatic!"

Abbi nodded dumbly, snatched up her envelope and ran back down the wide, echoing hall to the front doors.

But something the woman had said had warmed her heart. *You arts students are all alike.* All her life, Abbi had been singled out as weird, different, crazy. Now there was a whole school of people like her, and they weren't weird. They were 'dramatic'.

Abbi ran like she had never run before – her hair flying, bag bumping and her arms flung wide. How long would it take her to run there? The schedule said all students had to be in the school auditorium at nine sharp. Somewhere a clock was chiming. Abbi shut out the sound and kept running. She had to get to the auditions on time. She just had to get into that school!

☆ **CHAPTER TWO** ☆

'Hollywood'

While Abbi flew down the street towards the school, Jenna James was already sitting calmly in the front row of the auditorium. She checked her watch. It was just nine. Jenna had been one of the first students to arrive. Her dance tights were perfectly snug, her ribbed top perfectly smooth, her muscles taut and ready to do whatever Jenna asked of them. In fact, she was totally prepared for this audition.

She had been preparing for this most of her life, Jenna thought. Ever since she was five years old and had seen Karen Kain dance Giselle. Since that moment, being a dancer had been her only wish – on every birthday candle, wish-bone and coin thrown into a fountain. *I want to be a dancer* was engraved on her heart.

There were empty seats on both sides of Jenna, but the auditorium was filling up behind her. Not many kids wanted to sit in the front row, and that was fine with Jenna. They would just spoil her perfect focus on the stage in front of her. She wanted to hear everything that was said, feel every vibe from this school, before she had to dance.

"Jenna!" A delighted voice cried, and a boy slid into the seat next to her. "I didn't know you were auditioning for Holly! Cool!"

Jenna turned her neat head on its slender neck and glared into the brown eyes of Matt Caruso. Her face was perfectly calm, but inside she was seething. Not Matt! She had met him at a summer dance school the year before, when they were twelve. He was a talented dancer, but he wouldn't take it seriously. Worse still, he'd developed a terrible crush on Jenna and had driven her crazy all summer. Of all people, Jenna moaned inwardly, why did he have to show up now!

☆

At the back of the auditorium, Lauren Graham tucked her silky fair hair behind her ears and shoved her friend Martha forward. "Come on!" she urged. "If we don't sit down we're going to end up in the front row."

"I can't move," Martha whispered desperately. "I'm so nervous."

"Don't be nervous. You don't have to sing yet. They're just going to explain how things work and all that stuff." Lauren pushed Martha through the auditorium doors.

Why had she come? Lauren asked herself. She really had no intention of attending William Holly, or 'Hollywood', as her father sarcastically called the school, even if she did pass the auditions. No one in her classically-trained, musical family could picture Lauren singing something from *Cats*. They would laugh their heads off if they saw her here.

And her father would be angry if he knew she was auditioning.

"I came for Martha," Lauren reminded herself, straightening her slim shoulders. Her friend was hopelessly star-struck. She dreamed of singing on a big stage in a mega hit like *Beauty and the Beast*, but was too afraid to come to the auditions alone. She'd begged and pleaded with Lauren until she'd promised she would come with her.

Now, Martha was warm and sweaty with nerves, her curly hair bunched into frizzy clumps. Her face was red and her eyes looked ready to pop out of her head. She clutched her friend's hand desperately. "Oh Lauren!" she whispered. "You were right. It looks like we'll have to sit in the front. I'll die."

"I told you," said Lauren. "But it won't be so bad. Once we're sitting down, the other kids will just see the back of your head."

She pulled Martha down the slanting aisle to the front row and slid in beside a tall boy who was chatting to the girl next to him. He turned and grinned as she accidentally nudged his arm.

"Yes? Oh, hi!" he said.

Lauren's heart almost stopped. He had the warmest brown eyes and thick brown hair that fell on to his forehead, and a mischievous grin that lit up his face. She found herself staring at him and tried to wrench her eyes away. "Hello," she mumbled.

He grabbed her hand and shook it. "I'm Matt, and this is Jenna," he said. "We dance."

Lauren managed to glance up at him again. "I'm

L-Lauren," she stammered, "and this is my friend Martha. We…uh…sing."

"Singers! Neat!" Matt grinned.

"Be quiet," Jenna hissed at him. "They're starting."

As the auditorium lights dimmed, more lights came up on the stage. The chatter and laughter settled into a nervous, expectant silence.

☆

Abbi pounded up the stone steps and flung open the big wooden door. She looked frantically down the hall to the right and to the left. To her right, a teacher was gently closing the big double doors of the auditorium, holding them so that they wouldn't bang shut.

Abbi hurled herself towards him. "My mother!" she gasped, frantically making up an excuse. "The car…the traffic–"

The teacher shook his head and put his finger to his lips. "OK, just this once," he warned. "They've already started." He held one side of the double doors open so Abbi could slip through.

She stood at the back of the dark auditorium, staring at the lighted stage. There seemed to be no empty seats. Then she spotted one – way down in the front. She hurtled down the aisle, flinging herself into the seat just as a small, fair-haired girl stepped up to the microphone. She was wearing faded jeans and a sleeveless tee shirt. There was something familiar about her. She smiled and began to speak.

Abbi clapped her hand over her mouth. "Oh my God!" She gave a smothered cry. "It's Blair

Michaels!" She looked so much shorter in real life than she did on TV.

In the seat next to her, Jenna wriggled impatiently. How could she possibly concentrate on what Blair Michaels was saying with Matt leaning on one shoulder and this gasping whirlwind of a girl now sitting beside her. Jenna felt her calm confidence slipping away.

Blair was saying, "I remember three years ago when I first auditioned." She smiled. "I know how you are all feeling. This is the most exciting moment of your life…you can hardly hear what I'm saying to you. You've all got your music, or your dance steps, or your monologue running through your heads…"

Abbi suddenly let out a cry that sounded like a strangled cough. My monologue! she screamed inwardly. I've left it in the car!

Blair paused, glanced at the front row, and went on. "Some of you are so nervous you feel sick," she said, and there was a ripple of laughter. "Just remember, this is only one audition. If you keep on in the performing arts, you'll have many, many more. Some auditions will be good. Some will be awful. But whatever happens, as long as you do your best, you will learn something you can use the next time you audition."

Abbi's stomach started to burn and twist.

How can I do my best, she thought desperately, with my speech, my monologue, on the back seat of Mum's car?

☆CHAPTER THREE☆

The A-1 Group

Abbi's heart was pounding so hard by now that she could hardly hear what her idol, the great Blair Michaels, was saying up there on the stage. Her mind raced, trying to work out how she could possibly get her script!

She remembered placing the folder carefully with her audition script on the back seat of her mother's car, in case she had time to practise on the way to the school. Why, oh why hadn't she remembered to pick it up when she'd got out?

"This Saturday we will just be introducing you to the school," she heard Blair's voice through the fog in her brain. "You will each do a short audition. Some of you will be asked back for next Saturday. Those names will be posted on a list in the canteen at the end of the day."

Blair was smiling right down at her, Abbi thought in misery. She thinks I'm just nervous. She doesn't know I'm ready to throw myself into the orchestra pit.

"Next Saturday will be more try-outs – and more cuts. If you make it to the final auditions, two weeks from now, you have a chance to be one of the forty new students admitted to William Holly this year. If you don't, it's nothing to be ashamed of. You gave it a good try."

Blair gazed out at the full auditorium. "There are two hundred of you auditioning," she reminded them, "so you can see it's going to be a brutal process narrowing that down to forty. Now, look at the sticky note pasted under your seat."

There was a rustle and a murmur as one hundred and ninety-nine hands reached for little yellow notes. Abbi was too numb to move. She was still thinking about the audition folder on the back seat of her mother's car, at this very moment speeding to an appointment on the other side of the city.

One of the teachers came to the microphone to take Blair's place and complete the instructions. She was a large woman with a flowing dress and a deep, commanding voice. "The letter and number on that note is your group number," she said. "The other people with the same number as you, are your audition group – your life-line for the next three Saturdays. You will meet them after auditions, share your joys and sorrows, stick together and support each other."

Abbi could feel Jenna, the dancer, staring at her in the next seat. She jerkily bent forward to feel for the sticky note, and all her stuff slid noisily to the floor. She scrabbled desperately to pick it up.

Beside Abbi, Jenna glanced at the little note with the A-1 printed on it. She could see that everyone in their section of the front row had the same number – Matt, the human hurricane on her left, the small girl and her sweaty friend beside Matt, and a couple of other kids. Jenna smoothed her ballet top and let out a long breath. If this was her life-line, she would probably sink.

☆

"Now," Blair Michaels came back to the microphone, "just before you leave for a guided tour of William S. Holly, I'd like to remind you to talk to the other kids in your group. It will really help!"

"Hey, Jenna, talk to me. We're in the same group," Matt teased as they made their way back up the slanted auditorium floor. He did a little dance step in the air.

Jenna grunted. Matt's teasing drove her crazy. It made her forget all her steps. He draped an arm round her shoulders and she shrugged him away. "Cut it out!" she spat at him. If only he weren't in their group! she thought. Anyone but Matt.

Behind them, Lauren felt her face flush. She was also in the same group as Matt, but he wasn't dancing about that. She had a moment of pure envy of tall, willowy Jenna, with her cool, aloof air.

Abbi was at the front of the group. I have to get out of here! she thought frantically, as they shuffled slowly forward. I have to call Mum and get my script! She turned suddenly, and Matt danced out of her way to avoid being whacked in the chest by her bag.

"Hey! Watch out!" He put his hand on Lauren's arms to steady her. "She'll knock a little thing like you clear over!"

"Sorry, sorry," Abbi apologized. She wanted to scream. All of the kids from the front row were trapped at the back of the crowd.

Just then, a tall blonde girl elbowed her way past them. "Excuse me," she muttered, barging through.

That's the way to do it, Abbi thought, and head down, she followed the blonde girl through the crowd and out into the open air of the lobby.

The girl was hurrying towards the cloakroom.

Abbi followed. She had a shaky, sick feeling in the pit of her stomach. Maybe, if she could borrow some money to call her mum, there might still be time to get her script before she had to do her audition.

The girl was running water into the sink when Abbi burst through the cloakroom doors after her. "Excuse me," Abbi said. "Are you in our group? A-1? Because I wanted to ask you…"

Her voice trailed away. The girl had some pills in her hand. She gulped them down with a desperate gesture, then swallowed a handful of water.

"What?" the blonde girl challenged Abbi's startled image in the mirror. She had cold, ice-blue eyes. "What are you staring at? What did you ask me?"

"Oh…" Abbi stammered. "Just if…if you had some change so I could call my mum. I left my audition script in the car, and–"

"That's a good excuse for following me in here," the girl was still staring. "Mind your own business."

Abbi stared back into her cold blue eyes. "I wasn't following you," she finally managed to say. She was sure the girl had been taking drugs of some kind – why else had she been so anxious to get into the cloakroom before anyone else? It was filling up now with laughing, chattering girls. The girl straightened up, looked right through Abbi, and went into a cubicle, slamming the door behind her.

Shocked, Abbi turned and pushed her way out. She would just have to find another way to phone her mum. Maybe someone else in her group would lend her some money.

☆ CHAPTER FOUR ☆

School Tour

Tours of the school were organized by audition groups. The A-1 group – Jenna and Matt, the dancers, Martha and Lauren, the singers, and a skinny-looking boy named Dan – waited for their guide round a table with a big A-1 sign taped to it.

"I just came to help my friend, Martha," Lauren shrugged. "I don't really care if I get in or not." She was ready for the look of surprise on Jenna and Matt's faces.

"Well, it's nice to help a friend," Matt said finally, "but I don't think you have any idea what you're getting yourself into. These auditions are tough, at least the dancing ones are."

"They have to let me in here," the odd-looking boy called Dan laughed. "I've been thrown out of every other school for being the class clown." He made a gargoyle face. "I guess they figured I should train for the position."

"What do you want to do?" asked Matt. "You're not a dancer…"

"No? Check this out!" Dan did a comic pirouette. "Seriously, I want to be an actor. Today, my audition piece is from *Hamlet*. "'She speaks...'" He broke off.

Abbi came weaving her way frantically through the crowded canteen towards them, her face flushed. "Does anyone have some change?" she blurted. "I left my monologue in my mum's car. I have to phone her and try to get it back!"

Inwardly, Jenna groaned. What a bunch of losers! Class clowns, and kids who didn't care if they got in and...that girl!

Dan felt in his pocket. "Here," he said. "You're not having a very good day, are you?" He flipped the coin in the air, caught it and tossed it to Abbi.

"Thanks." Abbi shook her head. "Bad start, good finish – that's what my dad always says." She ran over to the pay phone on the other side of the canteen. Whatever had made her think about her father at this moment? His marriage to her mum hadn't had a very good finish. There he was, off in Australia, while Mum sold houses and tried to make ends meet.

Her mother's pager line was busy. Abbi tried ten times, but the busy signal still beeped maddeningly in her ear. She didn't dare to wait any longer – she might miss the tour. Then she'd never find the right place to audition.

When she got back to the group, the tall blonde girl from the cloakroom had joined them. She held up her yellow sticky note. "I guess I'm with you," she said. "My name is Chloe."

"That makes seven of us," said Matt. "Well, seven is a lucky number."

The school tour was conducted by a dreamy drama teacher called Mr Steel. Abbi was so entranced by his dark blue eyes and broad shoulders that she hardly noticed where they were going, as they went through the maze of stairways and corridors of William Holly.

"This is one of the dance studios," he was saying. "It's used mainly for classical ballet."

Jenna could hardly keep her feet still. The floor was perfectly sprung, the wall of mirrors and the barre along the side were glistening and new. She wanted to spin away from the group into a world of music and strong, beautifully controlled ballet steps.

"Look, we've lost Jenna," Matt laughed. "She's found paradise…"

Jenna whirled round on him. "Why don't you keep quiet," she blurted. "Just because you don't care–"

"Who says I don't?" Matt's grin faded and he stared back at her.

"Boys don't have to work hard to get into William Holly, there are never enough male dancers. But *I'm* going to have to work my socks off. So don't make jokes about it." Jenna said.

"Ahem!" Mr Steel coughed. "If you two have finished your little argument, maybe we can get on to the music room?"

Abbi kept her eyes open for a telephone as they were marched along the corridors. She just had to speak to her mother!

☆

The music room was lined with soundproof material. The ceiling was low, and a grand piano stood in one corner.

"This room is used chiefly for vocal music," Mr Steel said. "I understand Lauren and Martha are singers?"

Lauren felt embarrassed and she could sense Jenna was staring at her. I have no business being here, she thought. This is stupid. Mr Steel was waiting for her to say something. "Yes, I…uh…sing," she faltered. What would he say if he knew the truth – that she had taken singing lessons since she was six, that she studied with one of the most famous teachers in the city. Her parents expected her to become an opera star. They would be horrified if they could see her here! She really had to leave, now.

"Are the singing auditions tough, too?" Martha wailed to the group. "I'll never get through them, I know I won't." She was still clinging to Lauren's arm.

"I suppose it depends," Jenna said coldly, looking at Lauren, "on how important getting into Stage School is for you." Jenna was offended by Lauren's offhand manner. How dare she act as if it was nothing!

Mr Steel was looking curiously at them. "Well," he said finally, "on to the theatre. That's our last stop."

☆

The drama room had rows of carpeted benches like giant steps rising steeply from a small stage.

There was lighting equipment in the ceiling, and the whole room was painted black. "So," Mr Steel said, "where are our actors? Centre stage, please!"

Dan, Chloe and Abbi stepped out on the stage.

"Are you all ready?" Mr Steel smiled. "Monologues prepared?"

"Ready as we'll ever be," Dan joked. Chloe nodded calmly. Abbi felt a sudden urge to tell Mr Steel all about her horrendous problem, but he was smiling and turning away.

"Good. Well, that's our tour. We'll go back to the canteen now, and you'll wait to be called. You won't meet as a whole group again until three this afternoon. But we expect you all to help each member of your group auditioning in your area. You'll all need friends."

Abbi smiled at Dan, and he made a cheerful face back. Chloe ignored them both.

"Speaking of help, did you get your mother on the phone?" Dan asked, as they pounded back up the stairs towards the canteen.

"No, but I'll try again now." Abbi held up the coin he had lent her.

"I'll wait for you in the canteen," said Dan. "In case they call us while you're on the phone."

"I don't want to make you late…" Abbi began.

"Don't worry,' he said. "The ice princess over there will take our message to the masters." He bowed in the direction of Chloe. Abbi found herself liking Dan. He reminded her of someone from an old Marx Brothers' movie, all spaghetti legs and funny faces.

She tried to keep her hand from shaking as she punched in her mother's number. "Please don't be busy, please, please!" Abbi begged under her breath.

To her enormous relief, the line was clear. Abbi left a message: "Mum, I left my script on the back seat. I'm dead if you don't bring it here to the school. Please, please, Mum, drop the script into the office as soon as you can. Love you…'bye."

☆ **CHAPTER FIVE** ☆

First Try-Outs

"Did you manage to get your mother this time?" Dan asked, as they climbed to their seats overlooking the stage.

Abbi nodded eagerly. "I left a message. I just hope she gets here soon." Her monologue would be in only a few minutes. There were four groups of drama students gathered in the small theatre for their first try-outs

It was nice of Dan to ask, Abbi thought. Too bad he was so weird-looking. He was wearing, she noticed now, a black jersey, black jeans and black shoes. They matched the ceiling and walls of the small drama studio. "Why all black?" she asked, waving at his outfit.

"It's more theatrical." Dan struck a dramatic pose. "My monologue is from *Hamlet* – it's a dark and terrible tragedy. 'To be …or not to be…'"

Abbi slumped down with a sigh. "You dressed for your monologue, and I can't even remember what mine is about, and I don't have my script!"

"Oh, come on," Dan said. "It will all come back to you when you get up there. The script is just a crutch. You must know your lines…"

Abbi fixed him with her blue eyes. "What do you mean, *know them*?" she gasped.

"Memorized…you know, like learned them off by heart."

"Oh, no!" Abbi's heart was lurching around somewhere in her chest. "We were supposed to MEMORIZE IT? I didn't know we were supposed to learn it off by heart. The instructions said 'Prepare a Monologue'". She flopped back in her seat in despair.

Dan gave her a funny twisted grin. "I guess you haven't been around the theatre much…"

"No! I just want to be a TV star like Blair Michaels."

"She learns her lines."

"She does? I thought she read them off a teleprompter."

"Oh, you poor girl," Dan buried his funny face in his hands. "I think you're in the wrong place."

"No!" Abbi cried, straightening up. "I'm in the right place. I can memorize stuff fast. I can do it – I just have to get my script. Do you think they'll let me go to the office?" She jumped to her feet.

Now Dan was grinning. "All you can do is ask," he shrugged. "But the show must go on."

Abbi gave him a dazzling smile. "I know. I'll say I'm nervous and think I'm going to throw up. Keep my seat, I'll be right back…" She hurtled down the black-carpeted benches.

☆

Meanwhile, Jenna and Matt were warming up in

the dance studio. A nervous young teacher, Miss Adaman, was checking their audition order.

"You'll be first," Miss Adaman told Jenna. "Matt, you'll be after her."

"You're looking good, kid." Matt grinned at Jenna as she stretched on the barre.

And I wish you were in Siberia, Jenna thought. Matt had a real knack of upsetting her, and making her lose her concentration. Worst of all, he knew it. "Just get lost," she muttered.

Jenna felt the familiar trickle of nerves like an icicle down her spine. It was important to stay relaxed and focused. She knew her dance. It was a slow, floaty piece, where she could demonstrate her control and feeling for the dance. She had practised it for countless hours in preparation for this moment.

Jenna took her position at the end of the studio, waiting for the music to begin – a slow, romantic adagio. The pianist's fingers were poised over the keys. The first notes were struck.

But it was wrong – all wrong! An electric shock shot through Jenna's body. The music was much too fast! She jumped into the dance, trying desperately to keep up. The controlled, slow steps she had practised became the jerky movements of a wound-up robot.

Jenna couldn't feel the music; she couldn't adjust to the change in tempo. She was flailing around – losing it. She almost tripped over her own feet, trying to catch up.

The dance sped to a clumsy ending. Jenna

could feel tears of rage and disappointment welling up behind her eyes.

Now it was Matt's turn. He walked to the centre of the studio, spread out his arms and waited for his music to begin. Naturally, it was perfect, and so was his dance.

Jenna could hardly bring herself to look. Matt's dancing didn't have much feeling but it was technically dazzling. A glance at Miss Adaman's face showed how impressed she was. Matt had passed the audition, as if there was ever any doubt that he would.

He came up to her when it was over, wiping his sweaty forehead with a towel. "How was that?" he panted.

"Flashy, as usual. But that seems to be the style of the music around here."

"I'm sorry she messed up your music." Matt flicked his towel in the direction of the pianist. "It happens," he shrugged.

"But never to you, right?" Jenna blazed. "I felt like some puppet with its strings cut."

"Don't take it so seriously!" Matt's brown eyes glinted mischievously. His hair fell damply around his ears. At that moment, Jenna hated him.

"You don't take anything seriously!" She held her head high. She and Matt were almost exactly the same height, so she could glare into his mocking eyes. "This is more than just a game to me!"

"A game?" Matt shook his head. "It's not a game to me, either. If I was playing games, I'd be out shooting basketball or playing football with my friends. Instead, I'm stuck in here with Miss

Snobby, Know-It-All, Jennifer James!"

"You don't have to be stuck with me," Jenna snarled. "I'd like it much better if you'd just leave me alone."

"OK," Matt said, and he turned and walked away.

Jenna felt the tears prickle behind her eyes again. Why did Matt *always* make her feel like that?

☆CHAPTER SIX☆

I Can't Do This!

The throwing-up speech worked like a charm to get her out of the drama studio. Mr Steel had looked sympathetic and opened the door quickly.

Now, Abbi dashed to the office and hurled herself at the front desk. "My name is Abigail Reilly," she gasped. "My mother was going to leave something for me." This secretary was used to drama students. She didn't even look up – just shook her head.

"Sorry, nobody left anything," she muttered.

Abbi turned to go, then had a sudden idea. "Could I use your phone?" she asked. "It's very important."

"Students are asked to use the pay phone in the canteen," the secretary said, still not looking up.

"I know, but I haven't got any money, and I need…please…I think I'm going to throw up again. I need to call my mother."

Now the secretary glanced up sympathetically. "Try-outs are tough, huh?" She passed over the phone. "Here. Go ahead and call."

"Thanks so much," Abbi said, cupping her hand around the phone so the secretary couldn't hear.

"Mum," she whispered when the pager answered, "it's a matter of life and death. My script is in the car. I need it NOW!"

"Thanks," she told the secretary. "My mum's going to bring me some...stomach stuff. I'll wait out here for her."

☆

Back in the music audition room, Lauren crossed her fingers for Martha. She was going to sing 'Somewhere Over the Rainbow' from *The Wizard of Oz*. The music teacher was a big, red-faced man with flying grey hair, and a booming voice. His name was Mr O'Brien.

"All right...NEXT!" he bellowed, and Martha marched rigidly to the front. She looks like a wax dummy, Lauren thought in alarm. She doesn't even know where she is any more.

The pianist played a few notes of introduction, and Martha stared straight ahead, her large eyes almost bulging out of her head. But she didn't even open her mouth.

The pianist stopped, and played the introduction again.

This time, Martha managed to squeak out the first line. *"Some-where, o-ver the rainbow..."* It came out like a screech, but at least she was singing.

"And the...and the..." Martha had forgotten the words. "Dah-dah-da-dahdah," she sang, as the pianist bashed ahead.

Frantically, Lauren mouthed the words for her, hoping Martha would look down and see. But Martha was staring straight ahead, her face getting redder and redder, as she caught a word here or a word there. Finally she stopped.

"I can't sing this stupid song," she announced in an angry voice.

"Come on," Mr O'Brien blustered. "You can do it."

"I can't," Martha said firmly, and went and sat down beside Lauren.

Lauren felt an awful silence envelop the audition room. "Now, children," Mr O'Brien boomed encouragingly, "don't worry, Martha will have another chance. In the meantime, let's have the next singer, Lauren Graham."

Lauren had chosen to sing a song from *The Sound of Music*. It was very different from the German and Italian classical pieces she usually sang, and she had barely practised. She knew she would sing badly, but it didn't matter. She just had to get this thing over with.

She walked to the front and waited for the opening bars from the piano. "'*Raindrops on roses…*'" she began in a light soprano.

"STOP!" Mr O'Brien called from the back. "I can't hear you. Louder, child. Give it some gusto!"

Lauren was furious. The poor little song didn't need gusto. It was playful, and light. And there was no way she was going to strain her voice by singing too loudly. Her singing teacher would have a fit. She paused, and began again, a little louder, projecting her voice to the back of the room.

Mr O'Brien was looking happier, although still not satisfied. Every once in a while he would cup his hand round his ear as if to urge her to sing louder.

Lauren got through the song, walked back to her seat and sat down. She didn't dare look at Martha. The sooner they were out of here, the better.

But there were still six singers to get through. After Mr O'Brien's demand to "Belt it out", they all sang at the tops of their voices. Lauren shuddered, thinking about the damage to their vocal cords. Mr O'Brien shouldn't be allowed to teach singing, she thought angrily, he really shouldn't.

Martha had her second try at the end. She stood, swaying slightly, her eyes almost closed, and managed to get through the whole of 'Somewhere Over the Rainbow'.

"I'm so proud of you," Lauren squeezed Martha's hand as she collapsed in an exhausted heap on to the next chair. "You didn't forget a word!"

☆

Abbi paced the hall outside the office, willing her mother to appear. Even if she got her script right now, how could she memorize the whole thing in time? It was hopeless. She went to the doors to look out on the street and see if she could see her mother's car coming.

The street was blank and empty, snoozing in the warm sun. Suddenly, Abbi wanted to forget Stage School, forget the audition, run back out into the sun, as far away from William S. Holly as she could possibly get. All those other kids knew so much more about acting than she did – it had been a stupid idea to try to get in. Dan was right – she just didn't belong here.

What was she even thinking of, trying to be an actress? She imagined how embarrassed she would feel when they called her name and she had nothing, absolutely nothing, to say! She couldn't go through with it.

☆CHAPTER SEVEN☆

In, or Out?

Abbi was halfway down the outside steps when she remembered – her bag with all her belongings was still in the drama studio. She hesitated. Should I just leave it there? Who cares if I ever see it again?

Mum would care. The new wallet her mother had given her for her birthday was in that bag, and all her identification…and Abbi had already lost a bag in the past three months. Mum nagged her every day about it.

With a sigh, Abbi dragged herself back up the steps into the school and down the long hall to the theatre. As she pushed open the doors she could see Dan, centre stage, in his black clothes. His head was down, waiting to begin. She couldn't barge through the benches to her seat, grab her bag and get down again without ruining his audition. She slid into a seat on the aisle.

There was a single spotlight on Dan, making him seem like the only person in the room.

"'To be…or not to be…'" Dan raised his head and held up one finger. There was something so funny in the angle of his head and the pointing of his finger that a snicker of laughter flicked around the dark studio.

Dan paused, made a face at the audience that earned him another giggle, and went on. "'That is the question. Whether to suffer the slings and arrows…'" He clasped his hand to his heart and the giggles broke out into a laugh.

It was no use, Abbi thought. The more poor Dan tried to be serious, the funnier he was. The further he went into Hamlet's speech, the harder they laughed. By the end, kids were rolling off the benches, gasping with laughter.

Abbi could have died for him, but at the same time she was clutching her sides. There was no doubt Dan was the funniest person she had ever seen.

Finally, he stormed off stage, his face red, the gales of laughter following him up the rows of seats.

Mr Steel strode to the centre of the stage. "I think we'll take a short break," he said. "We've all had a long day. Abigail Reilly – you're next. Be ready for your audition in five minutes."

Abbi sat for a moment, collecting her breath. Auditions were terrible, even if you knew what you were doing. Pulling herself together suddenly, Abbi sat straight up in her seat, her chin thrust out stubbornly. I might as well try, she resolved. Whatever happens, it can't be much worse than what just happened to Dan.

She struggled up through the laughing, chattering students to her old seat. Thankfully, her bag was still there. Dan was hunched over with his head sunk in his hands.

"Hi," Abbi said.

"Oh, my God," Dan muttered through white fingers. "Did you see that?"

"Yes," Abbi smothered another helpless giggle. "Um – it was amazing."

Dan took his hands away from his eyes. They were bleak. "I guess once a clown, always a clown," he shrugged. "It seems I can't escape my destiny."

"I was going to give up and leave," Abbi told him. "I just came back to get my bag. I thought everyone else was perfect, and I was the only idiot…but now…"

Dan gave a lopsided grin. "I guess clowns are good for something…"

"No, I think what you made us see is how silly Hamlet is to take everything so seriously." Abbi shook Dan by the shoulder. "We were laughing at Hamlet, not at you."

"An interesting interpretation." Dan made a face. "So, did your script arrive?"

"No…" Abbi shrugged hopelessly. "And I'm next."

"Chloe, the ice-princess, is last up," Dan said. "Why don't you ask her to swap places with you? That would give you a few more minutes…"

"Do you think she would?" cried Abbi.

"Why not?" Dan shrugged his thin shoulders. "She's in our group and we're supposed to help each other, aren't we?"

"You're brilliant!" Abbi's eyes were sparkling.

"There she is."

Chloe was sitting alone in the front row. Abbi almost hurled herself down the benches. "Chloe," she begged, "can we swap places? I'm next, but I'm not ready, and you're last so I could have longer to–"

"No," Chloe interrupted coldly. "I won't change places. Last is a good position. The examiner remembers you if you're last."

Abbi stared at her, shocked. "You won't swap?"

Chloe just shook her head and stared down at her script. Her straight blonde hair fell over her face, hiding her expression.

Abbi made her way back to Dan. "It's hopeless," she muttered. "She won't do it."

"What's wrong with her?" Dan glared.

Abbi had an idea what was wrong with Chloe, but it didn't matter now. The five minutes were almost up. "What am I going to do?" She threw up her hands.

"I'll go and check in the office," Dan told her. "You get ready to go on stage. If your script arrives, I'll rush in and hand it to you. Reading it would be better than nothing."

Abbi nodded. Dan hopped over the benches in his comical, spidery style, while she made her way slowly down to the stage.

Mr Steel was there, with his heart-stopping smile. "Well, almost ready?" he asked.

Abbi managed a weak grin. "Almost…" she managed to croak.

"Don't worry," said Mr Steel. "We just want to see who you really are today, how you come across on stage. We don't expect you to know everything."

The lights were going down, the other students were taking their seats again, and still no Dan. But something Mr Steel had just said was beginning to prickle in the back of Abbi's brain. They wanted to see who she really was…

☆CHAPTER EIGHT☆

Quick Thinking!

The theatre was almost dark. There was a hushed, expectant silence. Abbi held her breath. Dan, she thought, you have two more seconds to get in here!

The door at the back of the studio opened. There was Dan's skinny black shape against the rectangle of light. Empty hands, and a sorrowful shrug. The script had not arrived.

An idea was growing in Abbi's brain. She let out a deep breath and began to speak:

"Dad, I thought of you today. The way you always said, 'Bad start, good finish' when things went wrong. I wish you were here, right now, because things are not going so great at the moment.

"And Mum, well, she doesn't mind that I want to be an actor. It's OK with her, as long as I get good grades and stay safe. But you, you would understand what an adventure this is for me…and you'd be cheering for me.

"Remember when you read me *The Hobbit*, where they all go off on an adventure to fight the dragon? Ever since then, I've been waiting for a wizard like Gandalf to come to the door and say, 'Abbi, today is the day you leave everything behind, and start a new life. It will be terribly risky, and you may not succeed, but you will see so much and feel so much and change so much along the way that you really must go.'

"That's the way I feel about being on the stage, and I have to do it, even if nobody understands. I've already learned so much, just by taking the first steps towards this life. I've learned that it's not all glamour and fame. It's hard work. Since I've never worked hard at anything, that's going to be tough for me.

"But I've also learned that acting is like a special club, that only a certain kind of person can belong to. It's like a secret society, and you need the password to get through the door, into that club. Already I know that the life on the other side of the door is what I want, more than anything.

"And, Dad, if you weren't so far away in Australia, I know you could help me find the password. But just knowing you're that kind of person helps me understand why you had to go and leave us, at least for a while. I never knew that until today. When you get back, we'll have so much to talk about. In the meantime, I'm going to pretend you're here. I'm going to pretend you're the Wizard, welcoming me to a new world. I'm going to think about what you would say, and what you would do to help me through this. Thanks, Dad."

Abbi bowed her head as applause broke over her and the lights came back up. She saw Dan clapping like a crazy man in the back row, and Chloe, white-faced and stunned, in the front.

"That was a very interesting audition piece." Mr Steel was smiling. "Where did you find it, Abbi?"

"Oh, it was lying around," Abbi felt the blood rush to her cheeks. She dashed back and dropped down beside Dan, her face flushed.

"You made it up, didn't you?" he whispered, grinning.

Abbi was still lost in the feeling of connection with her father. She nodded. "Was it...all right?"

"Oh yes," Dan smiled a big crooked smile. "It certainly was."

☆

It was a quiet, sober group that gathered in the canteen at the end of auditions. They were all waiting – waiting for the piece of paper with a list of names of those who would be asked back next Saturday.

"Well, Lucky Seven," Matt finally said. "How did you think it all went today?"

"Don't be so smug!" Jenna's dark eyes flashed. "You're probably the only one here who knows he's still in."

Lauren wondered how Jenna could be so mean to Matt. He was just trying to lighten things up. She couldn't take her eyes off him – the way his hair curled at the back of his neck, the way he moved. It made her want to dance and sing – her! Little quiet Lauren who never said boo to a goose!

If she didn't come back to Stage School, she'd never see him again. The realization hit her like a dunk in cold water.

"I hate this waiting," Abbi paced up and down. "It's torture! I wish they would just put the list up and let us out of our misery."

"You've got your wish," Jenna murmured. "Here it comes."

The large lady in the flowery dress marched into the canteen with a long piece of paper fluttering in her hand. "Your names will be in alphabetical order," she announced in booming tones. "Please do not trample each other all trying to read it at once."

There was absolute silence as she pinned the list to the cork board and marched out.

Then pandemonium, as two hundred pairs of feet stampeded for the board. Who was in, and who was out?

☆CHAPTER NINE☆

The First List

"I can't bear to look," Dan buried his face in his hands. "You go and see if our names are on the list, Abbi."

"I don't even know your last name." Abbi was dancing with impatience.

"It's Reeve. Dan Reeve," he muttered.

Meanwhile, Matt had somehow miraculously leaped to the front of the line. "You're in!" he cried to Jenna. "...and Lauren's in, and Chloe and me, and Martha and Dan...and Abbi! We all made it....!" he shouted, fighting his way back to the group. They threw their bags in the air and screamed and danced for joy; all but Chloe, who stood aloof, a strange expression on her face.

"Lucky Seven!" Matt whooped. "I told you we'd be lucky."

"I can't believe it, I can't believe it, I can't believe it!" Abbi shrieked. "We made it!"

"They must have taken pity on me..." Dan's crooked grin stretched from ear to ear.

"And me!" Martha threw her arms around Lauren. "I made it, too!"

Jenna's face was lit from within. She seemed to glow with joy.

"We should take down each other's phone numbers, so we can get together during the week," Dan suggested. "We can help each other rehearse for next Saturday."

"I'm going to need lots of help," Abbi agreed. "Listen – my mum's out all day – we could meet at my house." She wouldn't tell them about baby-sitting her nine-year-old brother, Joe, just now.

While they were scribbling phone numbers on envelopes and notebooks, Abbi noticed Chloe quietly walking away. She nudged Dan with her elbow.

He looked up and shook his head. "There's something very strange about that girl."

"How did her audition go?" Abbi asked. She'd sat through Chloe's audition in such a haze she hadn't heard a single word.

"Fine," Dan shrugged. "She did a scene from *Member of the Wedding*, where she played a kid who wants to go on her big brother's honeymoon. She was good."

Abbi couldn't forget the glimpse she'd had of Chloe glugging down pills with a handful of water in the girls' cloakroom. If she was taking drugs…Abbi shrugged off her uneasy feeling. It didn't seem part of this happy moment, this amazing world.

She walked out of the school as though she was walking on clouds. Her mother's little red car was parked outside – her worried face leaning out of the window. "I got all your frantic messages," she said, "but I didn't understand. What script?"

"My audition script!" Abbi said. "I left it on the back seat."

"Oh, Abbi, don't you remember? I tucked it back in your envelope. I knew you'd forget it."

"In my envelope?" Abbi stood in the middle of the street, stunned.

"Yes, love, take a look. It's in there with all your registration documents."

Abbi pulled the battered envelope out of her bag. Now it had phone numbers and names scrawled all over one side. She reached in, took out the wad of paper and there, on the bottom, was her script.

"Be careful, there are cars coming." Her mother waved her over to the car. "You're really going to have to try not to be such a scatterbrain!" She shook her head. "It took me half-an-hour to find you. I dropped you off at the wrong school. Were you late?"

But Abbi wasn't listening. She began to laugh. "I had my script all along," she gasped. "It was in here, all along! But it doesn't matter, Mum! I made it through the first cut." She knew her mother would never realize what that meant – what she'd just accomplished.

"So I guess that means next Saturday, we do it all again," her mother gulped. "Well…great!"

☆

"I can't believe you won't let me have the kids over to rehearse!" Abbi screeched. It was Sunday night and Abbi and her mother were having one of their screaming, I'm-going-to-have-the-last-word battles in the kitchen.

"You know the rules. No friends in the house while I'm at work!"

"These aren't my friends," Abbi corrected. "I hardly even know them. They're in my audition group for Stage School. We have to get together. Don't you understand?"

"If you hardly know them, all the more reason not to have them in the house." Abbi's mother was using her 'maddeningly reasonable' voice now.

"Then I'll have to go to someone else's house to rehearse, and I can't drag Joe along!"

Abbi's brother Joe sat at the table, stuffing peanut butter sandwiches through the gap in his space invader helmet to his mouth.

"You'll have to find another baby-sitter." Abbi's face was flaming and her blue eyes stood out in her furious face.

"Some of the people in your group are boys," her mother exclaimed. "You know I can't let boys in the house when I'm not here."

"Just the girls then!" Abbi pounced on the weakening note she heard in her mother's voice. "This is so important, Mum. We have to work together. If I don't see the kids in my group till Saturday, it will be like starting all over again."

"What do the other girls' parents say about this?"

Abbi thrust the envelope with the scribbled

telephone numbers at her mother. "Phone them. Ask them!" she pleaded. Surely other people's parents wouldn't be so unreasonable!

☆ CHAPTER TEN ☆

Getting Together

"I can't believe your mother phoned my parents," Lauren moaned. "Do you realize the trouble you got me into?"

It was Monday afternoon and Abbi, Jenna, Lauren and her friend Martha were gathered in Abbi's living-room.

"Lauren never told her parents she was auditioning," Martha explained. "It came as kind of a shock to them."

"What did you say?" Jenna gasped.

"I managed to make a joke of it," Lauren's face was pale. "I said I went to help Martha."

"What are you going to do?" Jenna asked. Her long, lithe form was draped over one of Abbi's armchairs. Her large dark eyes stared at Lauren. "Are you coming back for the second try-outs?"

"I'm not sure." Lauren looked down at her hands clasped in her lap.

"You're not the only one," Jenna shrugged. "My mother doesn't want me to be a dancer, either."

"You have to come with me!" Martha cried. "I can't audition without you."

Abbi dropped down on the floor, cross-legged. "I don't understand your parents. Why wouldn't they want you to dance and sing?"

"Oh, my parents, at least my dad, wants me to be a singer," Lauren shook her head. "But he wants me to study opera, not popular music."

"And my mother wants me to be a brain surgeon, or a scientist – something that helps humanity," Jenna explained. "She thinks dance is just a thing girls have always done. But not the way I want to dance," she added, looking defiant.

Abbi chewed on her bottom lip. "So that's why you get so mad when Matt acts as though it's just a game," she said slowly. "But I think he's more serious than he lets on."

"I don't want to talk about Matt," Jenna said impatiently, tossing back her long, braided hair. "I'm glad he's not here."

Lauren smothered a sigh.

"But how are you going to rehearse without another dancer?" Abbi asked. "And how am I going to rehearse without Dan? I need him to help me with my humorous monologue."

"Come on, we don't need those guys," Jenna insisted. "You can watch my jazz routine, we'll watch your monologue, and Martha and Lauren can rehearse their songs. Let's go!"

She unfolded her long legs from the armchair, stuck her dance tape in Abbi's tape deck and spun around the room. Watching Jenna dance was like watching the world come alive. Every part of her glowed with energy.

"That's great!" Abbi said.

Jenna stopped and put one hand on her hip. "That's just my warm-up," she laughed. "Wait till you see the real thing."

Just then, a helmeted figure dressed as a planetary invader appeared in the doorway, brandishing a portable phone like a sword. "There's a call for you, someone named Matt," a strange voice emerged from the helmet. "Do you wish to respond?"

"Yes, Joe, I'll get it," Abbi said. "For heaven's sake take that helmet off when you answer the phone. You sound so weird."

"I am not Joe. I am Ya-chet, First Minister from Planet Yex."

"Give me that phone," Abbi grabbed it out of Joe's hand. "Hi," she said. "Is that you, Matt?" She listened, nodding. "Wait till I ask the others," she said, putting him on hold. "He says we can get together at his house, Friday night, if we want. Food and rehearsal. What do you think?" Abbi stared around at the others.

A frown creased Jenna's smooth brow. She stopped in mid-leap. "The night before auditions...I don't know."

"I can't go unless his parents are going to be at home," Lauren shrugged. "There's no use even asking my parents to change that rule."

"Me too," Abbi nodded. "But I hate to ask Matt if his parents are going to be there. It sounds so immature!" She put the phone back to her ear. "Matt? We're thinking about it. Is Dan coming?"

Matt's voice sounded different on the phone. Younger and not so sure of himself. "Sure," he said, "Dan's here right now. He thinks it's a great idea..." Abbi heard a hesitation in his voice. "There's just one thing – my stupid parents will be at home – but they'll stay upstairs."

"Well, we'll think about it and call you back," Abbi said, grinning. She shut off the phone and turned to the others. "Matt's parents will be there," she laughed. "He was embarrassed about it."

☆CHAPTER ELEVEN☆

In Matt's Den

Lauren shut her music book and thrust it back on the shelf. There! Friday's practice was finally done. There was just enough time to get dressed for Matt's get-together before Martha's mum picked her up.

Lauren opened her cupboard and stared at it in despair. She had nothing to wear – nothing that didn't make her look like a little kid. That was the trouble with being so short, nobody took you seriously. The way Matt treated her, he obviously thought she was too young and too totally uncool to even notice.

At last, Lauren chose dark jeans and a black sweater. At least she didn't look eight years old in this outfit. She swept her hair up with a clip – that made her look taller. Now, she thought, if I could just find something to say to Matt. Every time I'm near him I just stand there like a stupid idiot!

☆

Jenna had stayed at Abbi's for dinner. Now they were taking the bus to Matt's house in town.

"Boy," Abbi remarked as they got off the bus,

"it looks like a tough neighbourhood."

Jenna shrugged. "It's not too bad – I live just down the street."

"Oh, sorry," Abbi apologized. "I didn't know you and Matt were neighbours. Have you known him for a long time?"

"We went to the same school," Jenna said. "But I've only really known him since last summer. It's not easy for him, being a dancer and coming from here. The guys he grew up with aren't arty, if you know what I mean. All they think about is football. Matt has to have a thick skin."

"So why do you give him such a hard time?" Abbi asked. They walked fast, under the street lights, towards a row of tall narrow houses.

"He gives *me* a hard time," Jenna said. "It's little things he does to annoy me, put me down, break my concentration. Nobody else can see what he does, but he's at it all the time."

"You mean Matt competes with you?" Abbi was shocked. "He doesn't want you to do well? I can't believe it!" She had to skip along to keep up with Jenna's long stride.

"You watch," Jenna said. "You'll see."

Matt's battered front porch was hung with paper lanterns. Inside, music was playing and the sound of laughter drifted up from downstairs.

Matt's parents met them at the door. His dad looked like Matt, tall and handsome, only older. His mother was pretty. Two little kids scudded down the hall to peer at the newcomers – Matt's brother and sister.

"Everybody's downstairs in Matt's room," his dad smiled. "Anna, Tony, show them the way."

The little kids raced gleefully down the stairs, leading the way to a part of the basement Matt had fixed up as his own special place. There were coloured lights, posters on the walls, and comfortable old chairs.

Matt's eyes lit up when he saw Jenna. "I was afraid you wouldn't come," he said to her. "Truce?"

"Maybe." Jenna threw up her head and just glanced at him as she breezed past.

Abbi shook her head. If Matt was just pretending he liked Jenna, he should be an actor. He turned and gave Abbi a sad little nod. "Did you two work hard this week?"

Abbi laughed. "We worked! You should see Jenna's dance…" her voice trailed off. "Is Dan here? I've got to ask him about my monologue."

"He's over there, searching through my music tapes." Matt pointed to a corner of the dimly-lit room. "He's been waiting for you to get here."

"Well, I guess we're the only two actors," Abbi shrugged.

She walked over to Dan. "I'm so glad to see you!" she cried. "I learned my speech from *Romeo and Juliet*, but I can't make any sense out of it. It might as well be in Greek."

Dan gave her his funny, lop-sided grin. "It's just all that old Shakespearean language," he said. "Once you translate it into ordinary English, it's great stuff."

"I'm glad you think so," Abbi sighed. "The only

part I can get is when Juliet says '*Dost thou love me?*'" She blushed. "Well, I guess anybody could understand that."

"We'll go through it tonight," Dan promised. "The Juliet speech is perfect for you. You even blush like Juliet when you feel embarrassed."

"I hate blushing!" Abbi said, feeling her face going even more red.

"Well, so does Juliet. She's worried that Romeo will think she's too pushy – that she's showing her feelings too much. She says it's a good thing it's dark, or he could see how red her face is."

Abbi looked around the room and laughed. "Just like this," she said. "Thanks Dan, I feel better…look, there's Martha and…is that Lauren?"

Lauren had come quietly into the room behind Martha. Her eyes searched for Matt, who was perched on the arm of Jenna's chair.

He gave her a surprised glance. "Wow, you look different! All ready for second try-outs?"

Lauren laughed. "I'm singing 'Tomorrow', from *Annie*. I'm sure the examiners are so sick of hearing that song they won't let me in for sure."

Matt jumped to his feet. "So you're still trying *not* to get in to Stage School?" he asked. He was smiling his wonderful smile, but his voice was sharp. "Some of us are killing ourselves to make it through the second try-outs, and you're trying to pick songs they hate!"

"I guess it's a silly idea…" Lauren faltered. "But you don't understand. My father thinks…"

"Who cares what your father thinks. Don't you

have any ideas of your own?"

"Leave her alone," Jenna said suddenly.

Matt turned on her in astonishment. "What? You're always accusing me of not being serious," he said. "What do you call this?"

"What you're doing right now? I call it bullying," Jenna said. "Lauren's just trying to help a friend."

"I couldn't have done it without Lauren," Martha jumped in. "We've practised my song so much I could sing it in my sleep."

Matt collapsed back on the arm of the chair. "I'll never understand," he muttered with a shrug.

"Let's have some music," Abbi said into the silence. She could see now that Matt could be a bully in spite of his smooth and super-cool surface. Jenna had a point.

"Speaking of fathers," Dan asked Abbi once the music was blaring, "what about yours? Did you make up all that stuff in your monologue last week? Don't tell me unless you want to..." He held up a hand.

"Well, it's true, basically. My dad left when I was ten." Abbi sighed. "I was pretty mad at him for a couple of years. Now I don't think about it very much. He lives in Australia. How about your family?"

"I'm the youngest kid in my family," Dan said. "My parents split when I was a baby and I've always bounced back and forth between two houses; sometimes I stay with my oldest sister. It's good training for an actor's life."

"You've thought a lot about this, haven't you?"

Abbi said. "Did you always want to be an actor?"

"Ever since nursery school," Dan said, "when I found out I could make the teacher laugh. Hey, want to see my Groucho Marx dance?"

"Sure." Abbi smiled.

Dan bent his knees and kicked out his feet in a comic imitation of a Marx brothers' movie. Abbi joined in. They threw themselves into dancing with such crazy energy that the others were caught up in it. The tensions of the evening relaxed. By the time Matt's parents appeared with a huge GOOD LUCK cake they were hungry, exhausted and happy.

"You guys better get some sleep," Matt's father advised. "Big game tomorrow."

"Dad's a football fan," laughed Matt.

And he'd like Matt to be a football player, thought Abbi suddenly. Even smooth, charming Matt had his problems.

☆CHAPTER TWELVE☆

Back to 'Hollywood'

"I'm so nervous!" Abbi was pacing up and down the aisle in the Stage School auditorium. This Saturday, the auditorium was only half as full as the week before. Only a hundred and twenty of the kids had made the second try-outs. By this afternoon, the group would be down to seventy.

Abbi and Dan had arrived early and were saving seats for the rest of the group. But Abbi was too restless to sit.

"Just relax," Dan told her. "Stop prowling around. You're making me nervous."

"Do you really think I can do it?" Abbi stopped and fixed Dan with her vivid blue eyes.

"Think about her motivation," said Dan. "That's the key. What does Juliet want in this scene?"

"Juliet tries to sound as if she's teasing, but she really wants to know how Romeo feels," Abbi said. "I read the next page. She even asks him to marry her!"

"You've got it," Dan laughed. "It was love at first sight…"

"I guess I know how that feels…" Abbi sighed.

As Mr Steel was striding down the aisle, he brushed past her. Just having him so close to her made her heart speed up. "I hope we have Mr Steel for auditions again," she breathed.

"Sorry," Dan said. "I think we have Miss Madden – if I can make her laugh, I'll know I'm funny." He pointed to the large woman in her long purple skirt and blouse. She stood centre stage, waiting for everyone to get settled in their seats.

"Oh, no…" Abbi gasped. "Is that Miss Madden? The one who wore the flowery dress last week? The one with the voice like a barking seal. She's awful."

"She's supposed to be a really good acting teacher," said Dan. "She was an actress herself when she was younger."

"Don't say actress," Abbi bristled. "We're all actors now."

"Sorry," Dan laughed again. "But can't you see her as an actress in the old style?" He threw back his head and posed with one hand on his hip. Abbi had to laugh. Suddenly Dan did look just like an old movie star. How could he do that with his face?

"Here comes the rest of the gang," he said, his normal self again, and a wide grin spread across his face.

Abbi whirled round and saw Martha and Lauren, Jenna and Matt coming down the aisle. For just a moment, she saw them all crystal clear, as if they were in a movie. Lauren, small and quiet, her eyes never straying far from Matt's face. Matt, teasing Jenna, who was trying to pay no attention to him. And Martha, clinging on to Lauren's arm, looking scared out of her wits. We all want something so badly, Abbi thought, and we're all afraid we won't get it.

She rushed forward to greet them, throwing out her arms. "I thought you guys would never get here. We saved your seats."

"Chloe's not here," Jenna looked round. "Has anybody seen her?"

Dan shook his head. "She'll probably show up in the theatre," he said. "Chloe seems to like to go her own way."

"Well, I'm glad we've got each other," Abbi beamed. "Here we go…"

Miss Madden was calling for attention. There was silence as she read out the schedule. "We should all be finished by three o'clock this afternoon," she finished finally.

"We'll see you in the canteen. Break a leg, everyone," said Dan cheerily.

"Never say that to dancers!" Matt called over his shoulder, as they piled out of their seats and up the aisle.

"Break a leg?" Abbi said. "Isn't that an awful thing to say to any performer?"

"It's an old theatre tradition," Dan laughed. "It's bad luck to say 'Good luck' to an actor before a performance."

"All right, break a leg, Dan. But it still sounds weird…" Abbi shook her head.

☆

The music studio was hushed and ready. The

teacher in charge was a Miss Shumacher. She sat at the back, writing notes on a clipboard.

Martha stood at the front, her hands clasped in front of her, her whole body leaning forward. Determination was written all over her face this morning. She would sing, or die.

Her song was 'I Feel Pretty', from *West Side Story*.

Lauren sat in the front row, her own hands clenched at her sides. She had memorized the words to Martha's song, and they had practised what they would do. If Martha had another panic attack and her mind went blank, she would glance down at Lauren for help. But Lauren didn't think Martha would forget the words this time. They had rehearsed and rehearsed until the words were coming out of Martha's ears.

The music began. Martha sang – better, much better than the week before. The trouble was, no one could believe that Martha did 'feel pretty'. Her face and body were stiff, and her eyes bulged. Her clasped hands jerked up and down as if she were pumping out the notes. Why on earth had they thought this was the right song? Lauren groaned to herself. Martha could look stunning when she was relaxed and happy, but now…

She glanced at the other faces in the room. No one was actually laughing, but there were smirks and a few raised eyebrows. Miss Shumacher was shaking her head and writing furiously on her notepad.

As she got further into the song, Martha slipped

off key. Come on! thought Lauren, clenching her fists tighter. You can do it! But Martha's face grew red, and her large eyes filled with tears. When she got to the line: '*Such a pretty face, such a pretty smile, such a pretty me!*' her voice cracked on the high note.

Martha's clasped hands pumped harder than ever. Somehow she made it to the end of the song, and then dashed out of the door of the audition room.

There was a horrible silence. Then Miss Schumacher spoke. "Right! I would prefer not to see anyone else singing with their hands held in front of them as if they had just captured a bug," she said. "I know that some of you have learned to sing that way, but I don't recommend it."

Now there really were chuckles and snorts of laughter around the room. Miss Schumacher held up her hand for silence. "The next singer will be Lauren Graham."

Lauren was furious. How dare Miss Schumacher make fun of Martha when she wasn't even there to defend herself! She stood up and walked to the centre of the studio seething with anger, waiting for the 'Tomorrow' music to start.

As the first notes sounded, Lauren saw Martha slip into the back of the studio, her face wet with tears. She knows, thought Lauren, she knows she isn't going to make it through these try-outs.

"'*The sun will come out, tomorrow,*'" Lauren sang, and suddenly she was singing to Martha, there at the back of the room. Soon, she forgot all about the audition, and the other people listening, and sang straight to her friend. It will be all right. Somehow, tomorrow will be better.

She had never sung like this. Before, singing had been just dry notes on a page. It was something she did as well as she could, but nothing she really cared about. But this – this was pouring out her heart through the music, sending a message she could never put into words! She could feel the whole room vibrate with her emotions.

And she could see that Martha was getting the message. She was smiling through her tears, and nodding. Lauren was almost unaware when the song ended. There were tears in her own eyes as she walked back to her seat.

She noticed a look of shock and amazement on Miss Schumacher's face as she sat down. What have I done? Lauren wondered.

☆CHAPTER THIRTEEN☆

Dance and Drama

"What's the matter?" Matt asked, peering at Jenna's tense face.

They were at the back of the dance studio, putting on their jazz shoes. Jenna was wearing a sleek leotard and tights. Her hair was pinned high on her head. She was about to tell Matt to get lost when something in his eyes made her stop. "Do you really want to know?"

He nodded.

"These people expect me to be brilliant because of my 'African heritage'," Jenna said bitterly. "It's so racist! What about my Spanish heritage, or my Norwegian heritage? Anyway, I love ballet a thousand times more than this kind of stuff."

"Hey, don't knock jazz dancing," Matt grinned. "It's what I do best. But sometimes I feel like they're looking at me and thinking no white guy can dance to jazz music. As though I have no right to it."

Jenna stared at Matt. This was a side of him she had never seen. She hadn't known that teasing, good-looking, self-confident Matt had another side. "Don't try to get me to feel sorry for you, Matt

Caruso," she said. "Come on, let's warm up."

Jenna did a ballet routine to loosen her muscles. She loved the way one ballet movement flowed into another, how dancers were always in control of every part of their bodies.

☆

Back in the theatre, Dan was on stage. This time, he was *supposed* to get laughs, and he did. He was playing Adrian Mole, aged thirteen-and-a-half, a hopeless loner, worried about his parents, his girlfriend, his zits.

The kids in the audition room were helpless with laughter. It wasn't just Dan's face that made him so funny, it was the way he became the character completely, body, movements and all.

He came back to his seat, grinning. "Whew, that felt better," he said. "Now it's your turn."

"But I'm not ready," Abbi said.

"Sure you are. Come on…you *are* Juliet."

"OK." Abbi took a deep breath. "I'm Juliet. I'm fourteen years old. I'm madly in love with a guy named Romeo, and I'm old enough to get married. I know it's dangerous to love Romeo because our families hate each other, but at this point I'm not thinking about poison, or double suicide, or any of that. I just want to know if Romeo feels the same way about me. Does he love me, that's all I want to know."

Dan was staring into her face. "I think he does," he said quietly.

Something in his eyes made Abbi stop and stare back. "So why is it funny?" Abbi's blue eyes were

☆64☆

wide. "I mean the whole speech?"

"Because she keeps telling him she has to go, and then coming back for one more minute. Because she's trying to act cool...and isn't."

"OK, I think I see," said Abbi.

"Just project what you really feel inside," Dan told her.

"Right. I'll think about Mr Steel," Abbi breathed. "I'll picture him, down there under my balcony. I wish he was really here, it would be so much easier then!"

Abbi didn't see the look on Dan's face this time. She kept Mr Steel's image in her mind until her name was called and it was time to walk forward on to the darkened stage. She kept it there through the monologue, and was pleased to hear little waves of laughter from the group.

"It seemed to go by so quickly," she gasped, when she got back to her seat.

"You were very good," Dan promised her. "Even Miss Madden was smiling."

Miss Madden had risen to her feet and was scanning the group in the theatre. "I have only one name left here," she said. "Has anyone seen Chloe Kaminsky?"

"I'm here," came a voice from the top row of seats. Chloe seemed to flow down the benches, her silky hair undone around her face. She had a faraway look in her eyes as she turned and faced them from the stage.

"Wow," Dan whispered to Abbi. "What an air head!"

"Be quiet, over there," boomed Miss Madden. "Chloe, we're ready for you."

She nodded, and the lights dimmed. When the lights came up on the stage again, Chloe was a teenager with a messy room, trying to find something to wear. She was in a mad rush to meet her friends. When an imaginary dog threw up on a pile of clothes on the floor Chloe made the whole room giggle.

"Wow!" Dan whispered again. "She's pretty good."

As they all filed out of the theatre, Abbi tried to talk to Chloe. "I thought you were terrific," she said, smiling. "Come and sit with us in the canteen while we wait."

"Look, just leave me alone, will you?" Chloe shook back her hair.

"Sorry!" Abbi said. "I was just trying to help."

"What makes you think I need any help?" Chloe turned to Abbi with an angry sneer. "And I don't need this group stuff, either!"

☆

Abbi nearly flew down the hall and enveloped Jenna in a huge bear hug. "How did your audition go?" she gasped eagerly.

Surprised, Jenna hugged her back. "It was better than I expected," she admitted. "I think I have a chance." She put her fingers to her lips. "Shhh – here comes Mr Rudolph. He was our examiner – he's head of the Dance Department."

The two girls ducked into an alcove in the hall as Mr Rudolph swept past. He was talking eagerly to Miss Adaman, the younger dance instructor. "So...the boy is not perfect..." he boomed in his Russian accent. "So he doesn't work very hard. I understand what you are saying. But how many young men do we have in the programme? That is the question I am asking you. We need a balance of male and female. I say we let him in."

And they swept off down the hall.

Jenna turned a bleak face to Abbi. "I bet they were talking about Matt. You see what I mean?" she stormed. "Oh, and to think I was actually feeling sorry for him this morning!" She laughed bitterly. "He's in – just like that!" And she snapped her fingers angrily.

"Are you going to tell him?" Abbi gasped.

"No! And don't you tell him, either. At least he should sweat it out like the rest of us."

☆CHAPTER FOURTEEN☆

The Second List

By the end of the day, the tension in the canteen was electric. Nobody needed to tell the one hundred and twenty kids in there that they were waiting for a list to be tacked on the bulletin board. Each time the door opened, everybody jumped.

At one of the tables, the A-1 group waited, without talking.

Matt was tearing a plastic cup into tiny pieces. Jenna was standing at the end of the table going up and down on her toes. Martha was sitting close to Lauren, staring blankly. Dan was rolling his neck from side to side, rotating his shoulders and cracking his knuckles. And Abbi, unable to sit still, was circling the table like a caged animal.

"Anyone seen Chloe?" muttered Matt.

"No. As usual, our mystery woman is nowhere to be found." Dan glanced up. "I really think she's on something."

Abbi stopped pacing. Had Dan guessed?

"What do you mean?" Jenna said harshly. "Drugs?"

"Hey, I was half kidding," said Dan. "I mean,

I don't have any evidence, but she's just too calm to be real. And her eyes have this weird, unfocused look…"

Abbi wondered again if she should say something about seeing Chloe in the cloakroom, but Jenna butted in.

"Maybe the poor girl is just trying to concentrate. Some of us do, you know. What's she like on stage?"

"Fine," Dan shrugged.

"Well, you shouldn't start rumours like that," said Jenna firmly. "Just because Chloe doesn't want to be friendly, and seems distant, doesn't mean she's high."

Dan gave Jenna his twisted grin. "You're right, and I was wrong. I will never say another word about our lovely Chloe, so help me."

Abbi sighed. Jenna was right. She shouldn't add to the rumour either. Whatever Chloe did was her own business.

Abbi stopped pacing for a moment and stared at her group. Here they were, bickering about Chloe, when maybe after today they'd never see her again. Maybe she, Abbi, would never see Jenna, or Dan or Matt, or any of them, ever again. Maybe she'd never set foot in this room again. She suddenly felt light-headed.

"Abbi, what's wrong?" Jenna said impatiently. "You're as white as a sheet."

"I…uh," Abbi stammered. "It's nothing." She dropped down on the bench beside Dan and wished the list would never appear. Until it did, they were all together, and she was still part of the whole thing.

"You probably haven't eaten anything since breakfast," Dan said, giving her a kindly pat on the back. "Want a coke?"

"No time," Abbi said breathlessly. "Here comes the list."

It was Mr Rudolph who came through the door and pinned the piece of paper to the board. He held up his hand to stop the rush. "One moment, please! If your name appears on this list," his voice echoed across the canteen, "you are requested to appear for the third and final audition next Saturday. If not, we hope you will try again next year, and keep on with your good work."

Mr Rudolph stopped, and coughed. "Now. If you are a dance or drama student, you will see a name beside your own. That will be your partner for the final try-outs. There will be no substitutions or swapping of partners, so please don't ask." He nodded, turned sharply and went out through the swing doors.

This time, the whole group surged forward as one body. Their eyes flicked down the list.

Lauren Graham. Chloe Kaminsky. Jenna James. Matt Caruso. Dan Reeve. Abigail Reilly. They were all there – all but the last name, Martha Turner. No one spoke. There was a stifled sob from Martha and Lauren led her away.

Out of the corner of her eye, Abbi saw Jenna's tawny face suddenly become pale. Matt's name was down as her partner. She looked back at her own name and felt the bottom fall out of her stomach. Her partner was Chloe! Who had made these horrible partnerships?

But right now, it was Martha who mattered. They all straggled back to their table to comfort her.

"It's all right," Martha said sorrowfully, "I knew I wouldn't get in. Now I just want to go home…" She turned her back on them, hiding her face.

"Good luck, Martha," Jenna said kindly.

"You're a trouper," Dan called after her. "I'm really sorry."

"Wait for me," Lauren looked sad and relieved at the same time, "I'm coming, too…" She smiled round at the group. "I'm glad the rest of you made it." She glanced at Matt. "I hope I see you again, sometime."

Matt's head shot up. "You mean you're dropping out?" He stared at Lauren in disbelief.

"Well…yes," she shrugged. "I only came because I wanted to help Martha. Now that she's not in…"

"That's disgusting!" Matt cried. "I hope you realize you just took the place of someone who cared about getting into Stage School!"

Martha turned back to the table. She took a deep breath and swallowed the tears that threatened to spill down her cheeks. "Matt's right," she whispered. "Somebody else here didn't get in because you did."

"Well, I'm sorry!" Lauren could feel the colour rising in her cheeks.

"But it's more than that," Martha clutched her friend's arm. "They didn't hear you sing. I did. You sing better than anyone else in here. You already know that. But today, when you were singing to me...I've never heard anyone sing like that. You can't drop out now, Lauren. You have to stay in, for both of us." She gave Lauren's arm a squeeze and headed quickly for the door.

Lauren stayed behind for a moment. She glanced at Matt again. It was not just that she had lost his respect, she'd really felt something when she was singing today that she'd never felt before. But what would she say to her family? "I'll think about it..." she muttered.

"Oh, spare us the sacrifice," said Matt sarcastically.

"You can talk," Jenna muttered to him. "She's not the only one who took someone else's place."

"What are you talking about?" He stared at her.

Abbi jumped in. "Why don't we all get together at my place tonight?" she suggested quickly. "I'm sure Mum won't mind."

☆ **CHAPTER FIFTEEN** ☆

At Abbi's

When Abbi got home, there was no one to celebrate with her. Her mother had sped off to her next appointment, and Joe was still at the baby-sitter's.

None of her other friends would understand what this day had meant to her. Abbi felt a great hollow pit inside. Then she noticed an envelope on the table near the front door. The stamp showed a brightly coloured fish on a blue background. Abbi felt her heart start to pound as she picked up the letter.

It was from Australia, and it was addressed to her! With trembling fingers she ripped it open and smoothed out the folded paper:

Dear Abbi,

I know it's been a long time since you've heard from your dear old dad.

But I just had the strangest experience. I was out on the Great Barrier Reef, doing some snorkelling, and I was down there looking at all the bright, colourful fish, having the time of my life, when all of a sudden, one of the fish reminded me so much of my bright, beautiful daughter Abbi that I almost choked on my snorkel.

It was as if I got a message from you – I know that sounds crazy, and I hope you don't mind being compared to a tropical fish, but I thought I should just drop you a line to tell you that I'm doing OK, and that I often think of you and Mum and Joe, and wonder how you're all doing.

And, just in case you want to write, I'm sending you my address. I'll be here for a month or so.

Then there was an address, and his signature. That was all.

Abbi sat and gazed at the letter in her hand. A big part of her was still angry at how he had treated her mum. Here he was, having fun in Australia, while they ate macaroni cheese and Mum worked her socks off.

But now, somehow, she wished he was here. She hugged the letter to her chest and danced around the empty hall. He would dance with her if he knew she made it through the second try-outs. She would write and tell him – before she started getting things ready for the party.

☆

"Joe! Stop eating the popcorn!" Abbi zoomed down on her little brother. "You're going to eat everything before they get here."

"If anyone *comes* to your dumb party." Joe scooted out from under Abbi's reach, scattering popcorn in all directions.

If only she could get rid of him! Abbi gave a huge sigh and collapsed on the couch. Her mother had called to say she was running late and wouldn't be home for an hour. They would have had some privacy, but not with Joe hanging around!

The doorbell buzzed and Joe beat her to the intercom. "*Who?*" he screeched to the voice on the other end.

Abbi could hear Dan's voice crackling over the intercom. "Let them in!" she hissed. She made a grab for Joe's arm.

"Are you sure?" He wrinkled his nose. "It sounded like some guy..." He punched the intercom button and wriggled out of Abbi's grip. "OK, come on up, but I hope you're not a vacuum cleaner salesman." He giggled fiendishly and ran off down the hall to his room.

Abbi danced on her toes, waiting to open the door.

It was Dan and Matt. "Are we the first here?" Matt peered past Abbi.

"Jenna hasn't come yet," Abbi rolled her eyes, "if that's what you mean."

He nodded. His teasing eyes were serious. "She's probably furious because they chose me to be her partner next week," he said.

☆

A street away, Jenna paced up and down the

pavement. She had seen Matt and Dan go in, just ahead of her. I don't want to see Matt, Jenna thought. I don't want to see him, or dance with him, or talk to him! She threw back her proud head. Matt would have an idea for their dance – an idea that would make him look good, and her look bad.

Why had Mr Rudolph and Miss Adaman put them together? How was she ever going to work with him? Jenna shivered, even though the summer evening was warm. She wished she had someone to talk to – even Abbi or Lauren, who knew nothing about dance.

☆

Lauren leaned on her piano, picking out a sad little tune. As usual, everyone in her family was busy with their own concerns. Her mother and father were practising a violin and flute duet, and her older brother Robert was pounding out scales on another piano at the far end of the house.

Her home, that had always seemed so warm and complete, felt suddenly empty. "I miss them," Lauren sighed. She could picture Abbi and Jenna, Matt and Dan at the party, celebrating. It was all mixed up in Lauren's head; she liked Matt, and she had liked herself, singing today. Everything about the Stage School gave her this fizzy feeling, like the first time she had tasted champagne.

But how could she walk into her parents' studio, interrupt their practice and say, "I want to go to a party at Abbi's." They would want to know who Abbi was, and where Lauren had met her and then the whole Stage School thing would come out.

Lauren played a few more soft notes on the piano. Then she got up, straightened her shoulders, and without thinking about what she was doing marched to the studio. She opened the door and walked round in front of her parents. They played on to the end of the passage then stopped, and looked at her with mildly curious eyes.

"I'd like to go and visit a friend tonight," Lauren gulped. "Her name's Abbi and I met her at my music lesson. It will just be for a couple of hours – I'll be back before dark." This wasn't all lies, Lauren thought, although it wasn't exactly the truth.

"That's fine, dear," her mother's eyes had already strayed back to the sheets of music on the stand. "Ask Robert if he'll give you a lift."

That was easy! Lauren breathed a huge sigh of relief. Robert owed her a jar full of favours – he wouldn't ask too many questions about what she was doing, she was sure.

☆

Abbi opened the door, beaming. "Hi, Jenna! I'm so glad you could come," she said.

"Look who I met downstairs," Jenna pulled Lauren in behind her.

In an instant, Lauren was surrounded by Abbi, Matt and Dan. "You're going to stay in?" Abbi jumped up and down. "That's great!"

"I knew you couldn't live without us," Dan joked.

Matt's smile was what Lauren had been waiting for. "One more week," he grinned. "Next Saturday it is!"

☆ CHAPTER SIXTEEN ☆

One More Week

"Stop, Joe!" Abbi cried. "That's Blair Michaels!"

Joe was flipping through the TV channels with the remote control. "Yuk! Stupid old Blair Michaels – who wants to see her?"

"I do!" Abbi wrestled with Joe for the controls and finally wrenched it out of his hands. "I just want to watch it for a few minutes."

Abbi found the channel. Blair, as the character Jackie in *My Life*, was walking down the school corridor with her friends, laughing and talking. She was thin and beautiful and had gorgeous clothes. But there was more. Blair's a good actor, Abbi thought. You can see her feelings in her eyes. You can see how she really likes Dylan, but she doesn't want him to know. How does she do that?

Abbi threw herself back on the couch in despair. It was Monday morning. How was she ever going to learn to be an actress like Blair Michaels between now and next Saturday?

She punched the cushion in frustration. They had to do an 'improv' next Saturday – and she didn't even know what 'improv' meant! She needed Dan.

"Here!" Abbi flung the remote control back to Joe. "Watch whatever you want." She picked up the telephone and paged her mother.

"Abbi?" her mother's voice came anxiously over the phone. "I'm showing a house to a client…what is it?"

"I need to rehearse with a guy in my group," Abbi pleaded. "His name is Dan. Please, Mum, can I have him over, with Jenna and Lauren?"

"Just a minute," her mum said, and Abbi found herself on hold. When her mother's voice came back it was low and tense. "I'm sorry, Abbi – no boys in the house. That's the rule, and it's final. I'll talk to you later. 'Bye."

Abbi hurled the phone at the couch and stamped around the small living-room. "What am I going to do?" she glared at Joe. "I can't leave you here and go to someone else's place."

"What did Mum say?" asked Joe.

"No guys in the house," Abbi groaned. "She's so narrow-minded!"

"Why don't you get them over and stay outside?" Joe muttered, still flipping through the channels.

"You mean like on the street?" Abbi snarled. "We live in an apartment block, remember?"

"What about that little place behind the building where I tried to build a fort?" Joe asked, not taking his eyes from the TV.

"The courtyard?" Abbi suddenly had a vision of the small enclosed garden in the centre of the tall block. It had a bleak rose garden, overgrown pots and concrete paving stones.

"Yeah, nobody ever goes there," Joe nodded.

Abbi dived on her little brother and smothered him in a hug. "Joe, my little genius!" she exclaimed.

"I'm not Joe, I keep telling you. I'm Ya-chet. Remember?" he said, stuffing his mouth with cheese and onion crisps.

"Where did I put that phone?" Abbi rummaged on the couch, searching for the portable.

☆

"This is amazing." Matt stared round the neglected courtyard.

"Are you sure it's all right if we rehearse here?" Jenna had brought a cassette player for her dance music and Lauren's songs. Dan had arrived with a bag full of junk food. Lauren had brought bottled water and cans of coke.

"No one ever uses it," Abbi flung out her arms. "They can't even see us here. All the windows that face this way are bathroom windows with frosted glass."

"It's perfect!" Jenna leaped on to one of the wooden benches.

"We can practise here all week!" Matt jumped up beside her. "Ready, partner?" he grinned.

Jenna's face fell. "Oh, that's right. I forgot you were my audition partner. How to spoil a perfect day!"

"At least you *have* a partner," Abbi sighed.

"What about Chloe?" Jenna asked.

"I got her number from the school," Abbi said. "I called and begged her to come, but she won't."

"I can help you with improv," Dan promised. "It's really easy. You already did it when you made up that monologue about your father,"

"And I'll help you with some dance exercises," Jenna said, "so you move better on stage."

"I need that, too." Lauren spoke up. She was determined not to be jealous of Jenna. Just because she was tall, gorgeous, and Matt obviously adored her, was no reason to hate her. "I could help you with breathing exercises," she added shyly. "They're for singing, but they might help with speaking, too."

"This is a great idea." Matt leaped down and spun on the concrete paving. "We'll pool resources, and teach each other. We'll all get into Holly."

"You know that's not going to happen," Jenna stared at him. "They're going to cut almost half of us next Saturday."

"That doesn't mean all five of us can't make it," said Abbi, excited. "Not if we work together, as a group. How should we start?"

"We need mats so we can stretch out on the ground, and feel our breath moving in and out," Matt said. "That's the beginning of all movement exercises."

"Breathing, too," Lauren nodded. "Your breath is your spirit. You have to let it out to speak or sing."

Matt smiled at Lauren. She could feel herself melting into the hard concrete. He looked so...adorable when he smiled like that.

"I'll come up and help you with the mats, Abbi," he said, jumping down off the bench.

"Sorry, no guys in the house," Abbi shook her head. "I'll get killed if I let you in."

"I'll help bring down the mats," said Jenna.

"Me, too," Lauren followed them through the back door of Abbi's building.

"I'm glad to have a chance to talk to you without the boys," Jenna said as they ran up the stairs. "I'm really worried about being Matt's partner."

"What's the matter?" Lauren looked at her curiously.

"I just wish I could be sure he wasn't competing with me," said Jenna, doing a pirouette ahead of them on the stairs.

"You don't think he means it when he says he wants us all to get into Stage School?" Lauren was shocked.

"I wish I believed it," Jenna said. "I wish I could trust him."

Lauren cleared her throat. "I've seen you dance," she said. "You're wonderful. I don't think you should worry about Matt. Just be yourself like you danced last week when we were rehearsing."

"And in the meantime," said Abbi, "do you think you could show us how to walk like you and stand like you? I feel as if I flop all over the place."

"And I look like a scared mouse all the time," Lauren laughed. "We really need some lessons."

Jenna's smile transformed her face. "You know, you two are right!" She laughed and shook her head. "Why do I waste so much time on that guy? I've got better things to do. All right you two – you're going to move like silk before this week is over!"

☆ CHAPTER SEVENTEEN ☆

In the Courtyard

"Abbi, you disobeyed me. I saw those boys leaving as I drove up." Abbi's mother burst into the living-room, her face scarlet with anger.

Abbi jumped up from the couch. "They weren't inside, I swear!" she cried. "We spent the whole day rehearsing in the courtyard."

"In the…courtyard?" Abbi's mother turned pale. "You had your friends in the courtyard, downstairs?"

"Yup," Joe threw in. "And they had food and music, and mats down there to lie on…" he grinned.

"JOE!" Abbi shrieked. "We were practising breathing exercises."

"You were lying on each other's stomachs and laughing," Joe said.

"That was an exercise to build trust," Abbi tried desperately to explain. "You each lay your head on another person's stomach, in a sort of chain, and then the person at the end starts a giggle, and pretty soon you're all–"

"Pretty soon we're all thrown out on the street!"

her mother cried. "Abbi! What on earth were you thinking of?"

"Well, we have to rehearse!" Abbi stormed around the living-room. "And I have to look after Joe, and you said the guys can't come up here, and Joe thought of the courtyard–"

"Oh, good grief!" Abbi's mum sat in the armchair with her head in her hands. "You remind me so much of your father sometimes." She looked up quickly. "I didn't mean that to sound…"

"It's OK," Abbi said. "I think I know what you mean. But you've really got to trust me, Mum. There's nothing going on. There's nothing to worry about. Lauren practises her songs – she's got a fantastic voice, and she's teaching us all how to breathe and talk properly. And Matt and Jenna are working out their dance routine, and teaching us how to move on stage. And Dan and I are working on acting exercises. It's OK, really."

Abbi's mother gave a huge sigh. "Let's have dinner," she said. "I have to eat before I can think straight."

☆

The next morning, Abbi's mother explained to the building Superintendent what was going on in the courtyard. The Super, Mrs Matthews, said as long as no one complained about the noise, it didn't bother her.

The courtyard was theirs.

"It's urban theatre," Dan said when Abbi told them the good news. "Five students seeking fame and fortune in a lost canyon among the city's tower blocks."

"Matt, wouldn't that be a good idea for our dance?" Jenna said excitedly. "We could be two dancers from different worlds, looking for a place to dance, a space in the crowded city. We could work in jazz, and ballet!" She grabbed Matt's hand, went on tiptoe on one foot, and laid her head on his shoulder, as graceful and beautiful as a lost bird.

Lauren felt a lump in her throat. It wasn't just envy – they looked so brilliant together. If Jenna was a swan, she was a humble sparrow. No wonder Matt never noticed her.

☆

"What's going on?" Lauren's brother Robert asked on Wednesday. "You're gone all day, every day."

Robert was the only member of her family who ever asked her direct questions about where she went or what she did. Her parents considered it an invasion of her privacy.

"I meet some friends...at a garden," Lauren chose her words carefully. "We're putting together a sort of street theatre thing – songs, dance, improvisations..."

Robert gave her a sharp look. "You're hiding something, Lorrie, I can always tell. Are you in some kind of trouble?"

"No!" Lauren said quickly. After Saturday, she might not even be in Stage School. But what if she *did* get in? What would she do? How would she explain that to her family.

Robert shook his head. "You look different," he said. "More serious...taller somehow. It looks as though my kid sister's growing up!"

That was Jenna's movement exercises, Lauren smiled to herself. She knew she looked different. She felt different, too.

☆

Jenna watched the city roll past the bus window on her way to Abbi's. Her mum had been giving her the silent treatment for two weeks now. Mum worked in the University library, and taught in the evening. She wanted Jenna to take science this year, not dance. Jenna's father had been a scientist. He had died when she was only four.

The bus pulled over at a stop and Matt came bouncing up the steps. When he saw her his face lit up. He did a little dance step in the aisle, clicking his heels together. Jenna felt a smile twitch at the corners of her own mouth.

"Hi!" Matt swung into the seat beside her. "I was just thinking about our dance. Maybe we should add a couple of lifts, near the end…?"

"Do you think you can hold me?" Jenna asked. She was beginning to trust Matt – that he would be able to support her in the lifts, and catch her in the leaps.

"All this practice is building up my strength," he said. "And we've still got two more days – we can do it."

☆

On Friday night, they rehearsed until the sun went down and their courtyard became a dark well. Now it was time to go.

They rolled up Abbi's exercise mats and

collected the rubbish and empty bottles. "When this is all over I'd like to come back and plant some flowers," Jenna said thoughtfully. "Those poor old pots look so scraggy."

Lauren began to hum. An old song was drifting through her mind. She remembered camp fires, and dark skies sprinkled with stars. With her body standing straight the way Jenna had taught her, she sang softly:

> *"It's a gift to be simple*
> *It's a gift to be free*
> *It's a gift to come down where you want*
> *to be.*
> *And when you find yourself in a place*
> *just right*
> *It will be in the valley of love and*
> *delight."*

Lauren's clear voice lifted the song so it echoed around the buildings that walled in their darkening garden. The sound died slowly away.

Abbi felt a shiver run down her back from the top of her head to the tips of her toes. "This is the place," she whispered. Their funny, ugly little courtyard had become a truly magic place.

"That gave me goosebumps," sighed Jenna. "I'll never forget this week."

"Tomorrow is going to be even better." Matt put his arm round Lauren's shoulder and gave her a hug.

"I wish you didn't all have to leave," Abbi cried. "There will be nothing to do but pace around my bedroom floor and worry now."

Just then, Joe burst through the back door. "Mum's home and she's brought pizzas!" he shouted. "She says everybody should come up!"

"Was my poor famished brain hearing things, or did your little brother say there were pizzas upstairs?" Dan did a comical mime of a starving man, tongue hanging out, stomach collapsed. Laughing, they gathered up their gear and raced for the stairs.

Later, while the others were wolfing down pizza, Abbi played back the messages on the answering machine. There were none for her. "I was hoping I'd hear from Chloe," she explained to Dan, when he wandered over to see what she was doing. "But there's no message. What will I do if she doesn't show up tomorrow?"

"I'll be your audition partner," said Dan. "We've practised together all week, after all."

"Oh, that would be great!" Abbi's eyes were shining. "I'd love it if you were my partner."

"That could be arranged." He gave her a mischievous grin.

Abbi felt embarrassed. Why did she always jump in with her big mouth? She liked Dan, but not in *that* way. "Dan– " she started to say.

"I know," he grinned. "You just want me on stage, not full time. Well, anyway, don't worry about tomorrow. I can fill in, if you need me."

☆CHAPTER EIGHTEEN☆

Final Try-Outs

The Reilly's little red car pulled up in front of the school.

"Well!" Abbi took a deep breath. "The next time you see me, Mum, I'll be a student at the William S. Holly Stage School."

"You know, dear," Abbi's mother said cautiously, "it won't be the end of the world if you don't make it."

"Mum!" Abbi stared at her mother. How could she even think such thoughts? "I'll die if I don't make it!" she cried. "But I *will* make it. I have to. I'm going to act so brilliantly today that they'll beg me to come to this school!"

"All right, Abbi, I'm sorry," her mother said quietly, "I just hate to see you get your hopes so high."

Abbi got out, slamming the car door behind her. Jenna, Lauren, Matt and Dan were already waiting for her at the top of the wide school steps. "'Bye Mum," she called, and raced up the stairs to meet them.

It seemed a lifetime ago since she had dashed up these same steps – late, alone, unsure where to go. In three weeks it had become like home, and these people closer than her own family.

They greeted each other with massive hugs, and walked through the doors as a group.

Some of the kids were standing in clusters in the lobby. Their voices were high and squeaky with nerves. Others stood alone, quiet and concentrating. Matt ran off to look at the dance schedule.

"I miss Martha," Lauren admitted, nervously. "I'm so used to trying to calm her down that I feel as if I'll collapse without her."

"Just hang on to me," Abbi grinned. "You can calm me down." She scanned the room for Chloe's tall figure and pale blonde hair. Where was she?

As if he read her thoughts, Dan muttered, "I don't see Chloe."

"I hope she doesn't come," Abbi held up crossed fingers. "I'd much rather do my improv with you." No matter what crazy idea Dan had in his head, she could follow him. It was as if their minds were linked.

There was no such link with Chloe, Abbi thought – just a high wall of hostility. It had been that way since the first week, since she'd caught Chloe gulping down pills in the cloakroom.

"Well, this is it!" Matt danced over to them, his face glowing with excitement. "We're first, Jen." Abbi could see he was dying to grab Jenna's hand and twirl her around, but he held back, respecting her space. He was learning.

Jenna gave him a startled glance. "We're first?" she gasped. "We'd better move then."

☆

"Jennifer James and Matt Caruso, are you ready?" Mr Rudolph roared.

From opposite sides of the stage, Jenna and Matt nodded.

The music began.

From stage left, Jenna slowly danced towards the centre. Everything about her body suggested loneliness, despair and longing. Her arms outstretched, her head bowed, she crumpled to the floor in misery.

Then Matt leaped onto the stage. His movements suggested fear and anger, the need to escape from the violence and confusion of the city.

Then he saw Jenna, in the garden. Together, they managed to suggest the small enclosed space, the safety and comfort it brought them, their joy in finding each other.

All at once, there was a new fear in their movements. Something was coming, from outside the garden – something huge and destructive. Their safe place was crumbling all around them.

Jenna tried to escape, only to be flung back from every direction. Now it was Matt's turn to sink into despair. Jenna tried to rouse him, to warn him of their danger.

The music built to a climax. The danger was close, the garden was being destroyed. Jenna fought back, but the walls closed in on them.

At last, they rose from the rubble of the ruined garden – as spirits, free at last. Jenna leaped into the air and Matt caught her and held her high as they disappeared from the stage.

There was no applause. For these final auditions, only school staff were allowed in the studio. But there was an eerie silence, as their pens flew over note pads.

Panting, Jenna and Matt stood in front of each other. Their faces still mirrored the emotion they had felt in the final moments of their dance. Suddenly, Jenna grinned broadly. "We did it!" she whispered to Matt, grabbing both his hands.

"It felt great!" His eyes lit up. "It was the best we've ever danced." There was nothing more to be said.

☆

"Lauren Graham," Mr O'Brien bellowed. "You're next!"

The singing teachers were sitting in a row at the back of the studio. Lauren saw Mr O'Brien, twirling his moustache, Miss Schumacher, her glasses drifting down her nose, and a third teacher, a woman with short grey hair who gave Lauren an encouraging smile as she stepped to the front.

Lauren shook her head slightly at the pianist. She had decided to sing without music. The teachers looked surprised, and then nodded. It was unusual, but they would allow it.

Lauren sang an old Irish folk tune, which was beautiful and haunting. She tried to put herself back in the courtyard the night before, and hear the notes in her head as she sang them.

"*My young love said to me, my father won't mind...*"

She could see Mr O'Brien shaking his head. When she got to the end of the first verse he held up his hand for her to stop.

"If you're going to sing without accompaniment, you'll have to sing louder," he boomed.

Lauren could feel her whole face getting hot. She straightened her back, the way Jenna had taught her and spoke very clearly and distinctly. "Excuse me, sir, but this song is meant to be sung softly. Besides, I don't want to injure my voice by forcing it. But I'm sorry if you can't hear."

She thought she saw the twitch of a smile on the face of the woman with short grey hair. "Please continue, Lauren," she said kindly.

Lauren fought her way out of the clouds of anger and embarrassment that threatened to overcome her – back to the courtyard at dusk, with her friends sitting around. She finished the song the way she had planned, with her voice drifting away: *It will not be long, love…to our wedding day.*

She opened her eyes and looked up. Mr O'Brien was plainly annoyed. The other two teachers were writing. Lauren walked quietly to the back of the studio and out of the door.

☆

"Abigail Reilly and Chloe Kaminsky?" Mr Steel shaded his eyes and looked out at the group.

Abbi was so glad it was Mr Steel. He would understand about Chloe not being there and Dan taking her place. She ran down the rows of benches and stood in front of him, gasping.

"Chloe isn't–" she began.

Just then, the doors behind her swung open. Abbi saw the light flood on stage, and when she turned, there was Chloe, silhouetted against the light, her blonde hair gleaming like a helmet.

☆CHAPTER NINETEEN☆

Out of the Frying Pan – Into the Fire

"Am I too late?" Chloe's voice was low and hoarse.

"No, Miss Kaminsky, but it was close." Mr Steel shook his head. "I'll give you and Abigail a few moments to get ready."

"We don't need it," Chloe was still trying to catch her breath. "Just give us our improvisation."

Abbi stared at her. What was she trying to do, ruin their audition? She could see that Chloe was nervous and jumpy, but did she have to be rude?

Mr Steel held out a bowl of folded paper strips. Abbi reached in and grabbed one. It said:

You are two fried eggs, cracked into a pan.

Abbi handed the slip of paper to Chloe. She glanced at it, and handed it back to Mr Steel. She didn't even look at Abbi. The two of them stood, side-by-side on the darkened stage, while Mr Steel took his place with the other drama teachers.

"You may begin," he said at last.

Abbi looked out of the corner of her eye at Chloe. This was impossible. Who would go first? How would she know what to do? Abbi felt her whole world crumbling, her stomach beginning to churn.

Breathe deeply, she remembered Dan's advice. Try to get into your partner's mental space. Be alive, be alert to everything she does. She took a deep, deep breath, and glanced at Chloe again.

Chloe was bending her body in half, tucking her head between her knees. She's making herself into an egg shape, Abbi thought, and followed her lead. As eggs, they toppled over and rolled along the floor.

Now, we get cracked, Abbi thought. It's my turn to do something. She gave a sudden, violent jerk, and toppled over the rim of an imaginary frying pan. Then she went limp, spreading and flowing out like an uncooked egg.

To her relief, Chloe also fell to the floor, following Abbi's lead. Now she began to stiffen, and twitch. Of course, Abbi thought – we're cooking. We're starting to feel the heat. She tried to copy Chloe's body movements. Her legs and arms jerked violently.

All of a sudden, Abbi was aware that something was very wrong. Chloe was struggling for breath – her teeth were clenched and her face rigid.

This wasn't part of the improvisation. Something awful was happening to Chloe. Her blonde hair was spread in a golden halo around her tortured face.

Abbi rose to her knees. There was something horrible in the idea that the people watching believed Chloe was portraying an egg frying in a pan.

"Help us!" Abbi croaked. "Chloe's – she can't breathe…"

There was silence in the theatre. They think I'm still doing the improv, Abbi realized. I have to get help, fast.

She stood up straight, her fists clenched at her sides. "Mr Steel," her voice rang out, "I think Chloe is having a drug reaction. She can't breathe. Someone should call an ambulance. She's not acting – this is real!"

She collapsed to her knees again, trying to calm Chloe's thrashing body. She's dying! Abbi thought in panic.

She heard footsteps pounding down the benches, the door banging open and someone shouting in the hall. The lights came on. Glaring and harsh, they shone on Chloe's pathetic body on the black carpeting.

She had stopped thrashing around now and some blood trickled from between her lips. Mr Steel crouched beside her. "She's breathing," he said. "Thank God. I think she's all right."

"All right?" Abbi shouted. "What do you mean? She's…she's dying. I saw her…taking drugs in the cloakroom three weeks ago! I should have told somebody!" Sobs were shaking her body now.

Mr Steel took her elbow, and lifted Abbi to her feet. "An ambulance is on its way," he said, soothingly. "But I think Chloe is just asleep. I've seen convulsions like this before, and I'm pretty sure Chloe has just had an epileptic seizure, she just needs to sleep now, and when she wakes up, she'll be fine, you'll see."

"But the blood–!" Abbi cried.

"She's probably bitten her tongue," Mr Steel said. He bent down to the still form on the stage, took off his jacket and draped it over Chloe. Abbi hid her head in her arms, shivering.

Now, someone else slipped a comforting arm around Abbi's shoulder. "What a *terrifying* experience for you." It was Miss Madden.

Abbi sobbed. "I thought she was just being a fried egg!"

"But you did very well," Miss Madden insisted. "You were alert, you used your instincts, and you communicated clearly." She led Abbi off the stage and out into the hall.

"Will she...will she really be all right?" Abbi looked back at the theatre door.

"Of course," Miss Madden said firmly. "We've had several students with epilepsy at William Holly over the years. It doesn't make the slightest bit of difference. I'm not sure why Chloe had a seizure today, but I'm sure we'll find there was a reason. Normally, if she took her medicine regularly..."

Abbi interrupted. "Medicine? Does she take medicine every day?"

"Well, she should," Miss Madden nodded. "Epilepsy is one of those conditions we can thankfully control with drugs."

Abbi was beginning to understand. The other students, who hadn't had their auditions yet, were milling around the hall, looking worried and unhappy. One of them was Dan. He shot a questioning look at Abbi and she shook her head.

"All of you might as well go to the canteen for a little snack," Miss Madden said in her firm, no-nonsense voice. "There will be a brief pause in the auditions, and you will be notified when to return."

Dan hurried to Abbi's side as she started down the hall. "Are you all right?" he asked. "You look as white as a ghost!"

"I'm OK," Abbi muttered. "I just need to sit down, and drink something. I can't stop shivering."

Dan's funny face was creased with worry. He led Abbi into the canteen and brought her a cup of hot chocolate. He sat peering into her face.

"What on earth happened in there?" he asked. "I saw Chloe run in just after your audition was called. A few minutes later people were running down the hall and shouting for an ambulance."

Abbi just shook her head, unable to speak.

Dan spread out his arms and paced round the table. "Talk to me, Abbi. I've been going crazy! Did you do your improv? Didn't you do your improv? Did Chloe attack you, or something?"

Abbi managed a pale grin. "You really do care," she said. "It isn't just an act."

"Of course I care!" Dan made a face. "I have to act my head off not to drool whenever I'm around you. But never mind that. What happened?"

"The improv is a lost cause," Abbi said. "And I probably won't get into Stage School. But compared with what might have happened, that's not important."

"Whew!" Dan flopped into a chair. "You'd better

start from the beginning. I want all the details."

"Save your energy for your audition," Abbi told Dan. "I'll tell you all about it later."

"You're right, you're right." Dan jumped to his feet. "I wish they'd get it over with. This day seems about a hundred years long."

A few minutes later, Miss Madden came swishing through the canteen's swing doors. "Situation normal!" she sang out. "Those of you who have not done your audition should return to the hall outside the drama studio."

"Do you want to come with me?" Dan asked.

"No," Abbi said. "I'll stay here and wait for everybody else."

☆**CHAPTER TWENTY**☆

The Last List

"I can't stand it!" Jenna cried. She threw up her graceful arms and did a complete spin beside their table. "This waiting is torture!"

"We danced well," said Matt. "Stop worrying."

"But maybe everyone danced just as well," Jenna protested. "Maybe there's some little tiny thing about me they didn't like – or they're trying to keep a balance, so they let guys in ahead of girls..." She stopped and turned to face Matt.

"Is that what has been eating you all this time?" Matt rose to his feet. "You don't think I can get in on my own merits – you think I'll get in just because I'm a guy?"

"I'm sorry, but you know it's true."

"It's not true!" Matt glared back at Jenna.

"Abbi and I heard...tell them what we heard," Jenna whirled to Abbi.

"Truce!" Abbi said. "Who cares. Matt's a good dancer, and he worked hard, and you know it." Abbi was surprised at herself. She hadn't thought she could stand up to Jenna.

"Here comes Lauren," said Dan. "She looks like

she's carrying the whole world on her shoulders."

Lauren pulled up a chair and managed a wan grin. "Hi," she said. "Well, I guess it's over."

"What happened?" Abbi asked.

"Oh, I told one of the teachers off, that's all," Lauren said. "I think I'm probably at the bottom of his list."

Lauren straightened her shoulders. "How about the rest of you? Did Chloe ever show up, Abbi?"

Abbi nodded. Sooner or later, she was going to have to tell them the whole story. But right now, she didn't feel like talking about it.

"I was brilliant, as usual," Dan shot into the waiting silence. "If they don't pick me, this school is not worth getting into."

"What was your improv?" Lauren asked.

"It was perfect for me," Dan laughed. "I was a dog, trying to get my human to take me for a walk. My partner is a guy in the theatre group named Mike. He did his best to ignore me, and then, when I finally convinced him I had to go, and he got all dressed and ready and found my lead, I wouldn't go out because it was raining."

"I can just see you as a dog." Matt laughed. "A skinny black dog with a long nose."

"Hey, it's not that easy," Dan shrugged. "You have to think like an animal." He leaped up on the table on all fours, panting in their faces.

But no one was paying any attention to him. They were all looking past him towards the door. Mr Steel stood there, a piece of paper in his hand, his hair dishevelled.

He looked as if he was about to say something, then changed his mind. Quickly, he tacked the list to the bulletin board, and left.

This time there was no stampede. They all moved forward slowly to read their fate.

"Graham," Matt read out. He was the tallest, and could see over the heads of the kids in front.

Lauren turned white, then red. "I – m-made it?" she stammered. "I don't believe it!"

"Kaminsky, Chloe," he went on. "James, Jenna!"

Jenna's whole body dissolved in relief. She grabbed Abbi for support, her face a mask of joy.

"Me," Matt bowed. "Reeve, Dan." He paused, and then beamed at Abbi. "Reilly, Abigail…we all made it, just like I said we would."

Linking arms, bursting with happiness, the A-1 group surged back to their table. Abbi felt the dark clouds of the day roll away. The impossible had happened. They had all made it into Stage School!

All around them were faces of disappointment and despair.

"Students whose names are on the list please gather in the auditorium," Mrs Madden announced from the doorway. "The rest, stay here for a moment, will you?"

"You go ahead," Abbi gasped. "I have to find Chloe. I want to make sure she knows."

"You're going to be late," Matt shook his head.

"What else is new?" Abbi grinned at him as she tore away.

☆

Abbi raced down the hall to the nurse's room, her

hair flying. This was where Miss Madden had said Chloe was resting.

Trying to calm herself, Abbi pushed the door open gently. Chloe was lying on a narrow bed, her eyes closed.

"Are you asleep?" Abbi whispered. "It's me, Abbi."

Chloe's eyes fluttered open. There were dark circles under them, and her face was still very pale. "I'm sorry…" she started to say.

"That's all right–" Abbi started to rush ahead with her good news.

"No! I'm so sorry for the way I acted," Chloe whispered.

"Don't apologize. I've got good news. We both made it–"

But Chloe wasn't listening. A tear rolled down her pale face. "I was so awful to you – I didn't want anyone to know I was…ill. That's why I got so angry when you saw me taking pills in the cloakroom."

Abbi took her hand. "Chloe, listen, it's really not important. We both *made* it. We passed the auditions! We're in Stage School!"

A look of complete astonishment spread over Chloe's face. She brushed the tears away. "We really *made* it?" she gasped, half sitting up. "Even after I messed things up?"

"You didn't– " Abbi started.

"Oh yes I did." Chloe held up her hand, sinking back on her pillow. "I'm supposed to take my pills at the same time every day. But they make me feel sleepy sometimes, and I hate taking them. I thought I didn't need them any more, that it wouldn't matter. They must have felt sorry for me..." She turned her face towards the wall. "That's why they let me in."

Abbi gulped. "I don't think so," she said. "You're really beautiful, Chloe. There's something about you that's..." she searched for the word... "riveting!"

"Do you really think so?" Chloe turned her head back again and smiled at Abbi.

"Yes, I do," Abbi nodded. "I think you're going to be a big star one day."

"You, too," whispered Chloe. "When you're on stage no one can take their eyes off you. You made me so jealous."

Abbi laughed. "Let's start all over again," she said. "If you feel well enough later, we're all getting together at my place." She scribbled her address on a piece of paper and handed it to Chloe.

☆CHAPTER TWENTY-ONE☆

Final Curtain

The chosen forty filed into the auditorium, and took their seats quietly. Most of them had left bitterly disappointed friends outside the closed auditorium doors, and they felt almost guilty at having survived the cuts.

Mr Steel strode on, centre stage. "I know how you're feeling," he said. "You don't quite believe you've made it. You feel very sad about the people who didn't, and it's all a bit overwhelming."

There were nods and sighs from the scattered audience.

"Move in!" Mr Steel waved his arms. "Move closer together in the front and centre. You're a class now – next year's Stage School's first year class." He came down off the stage as they gathered in the front seats, and stood in front of them.

"You're going to go through a lot together in the next three years," Mr Steel went on. He grinned at them. "But first, pat yourself on the back. Let yourself feel really, really great. And remember this feeling and this good moment. It will come in handy when things get tough."

Abbi felt an enormous excitement taking hold of her. This was her new life, the new adventure beginning. Everything would be different from now on. And on top of that, she would be seeing Mr Steel every single day!

"Now," he paused, "let me tell you what will happen in September. In the first few weeks we'll be casting the roles for our autumn show. So you'll be right back into auditions again."

Abbi and Jenna exchanged looks.

"That's right," Mr Steel nodded. "We want to make Stage School as much like the real world of performance art as we possibly can. That world is constant auditions, and lots of hard work, once you get a part…"

"So." He smiled his heart-melting smile. "Enjoy this moment and get ready for it. Auditions and rehearsals in September. The show in October."

There was an excited murmur from the group.

"And just in case that sounds like fun, don't forget you'll be coping with mathematics, French, science and all your other subjects at the same time."

This brought groans from the group of new Stage School students.

"You'll work twice as hard as other students your age, and sometimes it will feel as though your feet never touch the ground."

Abbi nodded eagerly. This was what she'd always wanted! She didn't care how much work she had to do, she was where she'd dreamed of being, doing the thing she loved best – acting! She

wanted just what Mr Steel described. He was right
– her feet would never touch the ground. She
would really fly!

Preview the next

STAGE SCH★★L

NOW...

Abbi – Blind Ambition

☆CHAPTER ONE☆

Blair

Abbi Reilly hurried down the school hall. She was trying to juggle an armful of books and read her timetable at the same time. Why could she never, ever remember what class was next? Or where the classrooms were in this big old brick building? Stage School was so confusing!

In Abbi's hurry, she tripped on a loose floor tile. All the books and papers exploded out of her arms and spread across the shiny tile floor. Abbi scrabbled to pick them up, gripping the timetable in her teeth so it wouldn't get away on her.

"Oh help. This is not happening. I'm going to be so, so late for French," she muttered.

Abbi's mane of golden hair swirled around her as she dived for her books. It framed a heart-shaped face with high cheekbones and wide-spaced blue eyes. Everything about Abbi sparkled with energy, but at this moment, she looked like a spinning top, out of control.

She had looked forward to the first week of Stage School so much – had worked so hard to get into the school. And now, she had to admit it – she hated everything about William S. Holly, or "Hollywood" as the school was often called.

She had thought Stage School would be a whole new world, where she would learn to act and sing and dance. Instead, the teachers were even more heartless and strict than in her old school. The timetable was so complicated that she hardly ever saw her friends Jenna and Lauren who had been in the same audition group with her that summer. And she seemed to be always late, and lost. Like now! This couldn't be the right hall – there was no one else here.

"Can I help?" A familiar voice made her look up with a start. A girl had appeared out of nowhere, and stood smiling down at her. She was shorter than Abbi, with short blonde hair and a lovely smile. It was a face Abbi knew so well, a voice she heard every week from seven to eight on Tuesdays.

Abbi blushed scarlet. She took the timetable out of her mouth and managed to stammer. "You're…Blair..." Blair Michaels!"

The girl nodded.

"You're my favourite TV star," Abbi gasped. I watch every episode of *My Life*. I think you're the best person in the show!"

"Thank you." Blair tipped her head to one side. "I don't think I've seen you before. You must be a new student."

"You don't understand," Abbi said, still staring at Blair with a dazed expression. "I'm here because of you. You're the person who inspired me to become an actress...I knew you went to the school and that's why I auditioned! You look...so different in real life." Abbi knew she was talking too much, but she couldn't stop. This was really Blair Michaels, in the flesh, having a conversation with her!

Blair laughed, a lovely, tinkling sound. "That's what everyone says. I look different without make-up on."

"No, you're just so tiny and...and like a normal person. I want to be just like you!" she ended, blushing.

"You do?" Blair laughed again.

"I mean, I really want to act!" Abbi said. "That's why I came to this school."

"Well, you picked a good place," said Blair. "Are you on your way to class? Can I help?" She pointed to the fan of fallen papers. "It looks like you've had an accident."

"Oh...I...uh...I was trying to find out where I'm supposed to be next," Abbi murmured. Her bright blue eyes were riveted to Blair's face. She held up her timetable. "I never seem to be able to work out if it's Day One or Day Two, or which period it is."

Blair waved a graceful hand. "Oh, you'll get it all sorted out, don't worry," she said, as if school didn't matter in the slightest. "Did you hear they've put out the casting call for *Dracula*?"

Abbi scooped up all her notebooks together in

one messy heap and stood up with a gasp. "You mean this autumn's show? They've called auditions, already?"

"The notice is up in the canteen," Blair nodded. She bent over and gathered up a few papers Abbi had missed. "Are you going to try out for a part?"

"Me?" Abbi gasped again. "Oh…I…yes!" She and her friends Lauren and Jenna had been talking about the school's production of *Dracula: The Musical* ever since the summer. They'd thought about little else except getting parts in the show.

"Good," Blair said. "What's your name?"

"Abbi…Abigail Reilly," Abbi stammered. She felt quite dizzy. Blair actually wanted to know her name!

"You have a wonderful look," Blair went on, "and I think you'd be perfect for the part of Lucy, the girl who gets bitten by Dracula. Be sure to try out for her and I'll put in a good word with Alan Steel."

Abbi's head was reeling. Blair called Mr Steel – the drama teacher and director of *Dracula* – Alan! Abbi had been crazy about Mr Steel from the moment she'd set eyes on him!

She stared at Blair. What must it be like to be her? A star with her own TV series, written about in magazines, appearing on talk shows, talking about teachers as if they were casual friends! It was everything Abbi wanted.

Blair gave a theatrical wave. "I've got to be going," she smiled at Abbi again. "See you at the auditions for *Dracula* then." And she breezed off down the empty hall.

Abbi sank to the floor again, leaning back against a wall of lockers. It was unbelievable! How could she go to French now, and sit at a desk muttering French verbs?

She forced her eyes to focus on the timetable still clutched in her hand. A glance at the clock told her it was eleven-thirty. It was first lunch period and Jenna and Lauren both had first lunch. They might be in the canteen right now.

Leaping to her feet, Abbi thundered down the corridor, her hair and book bag flying. Forget French! She had to find her friends and tell them all the news. *A wonderful look*, her heart sang. *Blair thinks I have a wonderful look!*

Why is Blair being so nice? She's a big star and everyone thinks she's great…don't they? Will she help Abbi get a part in 'Dracula' or has she got other reasons for being friendly? Read on in…

Stage School 2
☆*Abbi - Blind Ambition*☆

Have you read the other Stage School stories?